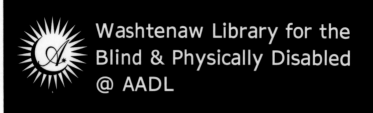

Washtenaw Library for the Blind & Physically Disabled @ AADL

If you are only able to read large print, you may qualify for WLBPD @ AADL services, including receiving audio and large print books by mail at no charge.

For more information:

Email • wlbpd@aadl.org
Phone • (734) 327-4224
Website • wlbpd.aadl.org

THE HITCH

Gerald Hammond titles available from
Severn House Large Print

The Dirty Dollar
Down the Garden Path
Grail for Sale
The Snatch

THE HITCH

Gerald Hammond

Severn House Large Print
London & New York

This first large print edition published in Great Britain 2004 by
SEVERN HOUSE LARGE PRINT BOOKS LTD of
9-15 High Street, Sutton, Surrey, SM1 1DF.
First world regular print edition published 2004 by
Severn House Publishers, London and New York.
This first large print edition published in the USA 2005 by
SEVERN HOUSE PUBLISHERS INC., of
595 Madison Avenue, New York, NY 10022.

British Library Cataloguing in Publication Data

Hammond, Gerald, 1926 -
    The hitch. - Large print ed.
    1. Fraud - Scotland - Fiction
    2. Celebrity weddings - Scotland - Fiction
    3. Detective and mystery stories
    4. Large type books
    I. Title
    823.9'14 [F]

ISBN 0-7278-7399-7

Printed and bound in Great Britain by
MPG Books Ltd, Bodmin, Cornwall.

One

There had been a time when an invitation to her father's study would have set Alice to examining her conscience in prospect of an inquisition followed by a lecture. The very prototype of mature respectability would have been about to tower above disreputable youth. Jove could have been expected to thunder. So it had been for almost as long as Alice could remember. The tenderness which had illuminated her childhood seemed so remote as to be almost a dream.

But not any more.

If anyone were entitled to occupy the moral high ground it would now be Alice, but only by the slenderest of margins. She had no intention of stealing that advantage. But for her father's quick thinking and personal sacrifice, Alice might have found herself at a similar disadvantage. The family reunion just concluded had not been the

5

jolly celebration that might have been expected.

Mr Dunwoodie had come home that day from prison.

The occasion had called for a subdued family celebration. Alice's parents had, of course, been present, Alice herself and her moderately respectable solicitor brother. Justin, Alice's husband of little over a year, whose own past had not been spent entirely on the sunny side of the law, was wary of being seen to associate too closely with a recent jailbird and had seized on the excuse offered by a client conference in London to absent himself, with Alice's grudging acquiescence.

When the meal was finished and a welcome home had been expressed and accepted in what amounted almost to speech-making, Alice's brother had escaped to join his friends in activities that Alice knew to be dubious at best. Their mother had retired thankfully to the kitchen. Mr Dunwoodie and Alice had adjourned to his study, taking with them, respectively, a brandy and soda and a glass of red wine. He settled into the big chair behind the desk as though he had never been away, leaving Alice to take the visitor's chair. In Alice's memory, he had passed from being the god-like father figure that she had adored in her childhood, through being the oppressive tyrant of her teens to become the prisoner to be visited, blustering to conceal his feelings of shame. Now, it seemed, he had shed all those guises and was simply being himself and she found herself prepared to like him better.

The room also had seemed to change from something between a head teacher's study and a court of law and into a pleasant but undistinguished room furnished with no more than a desk, some assorted chairs and a bookcase that held more sporting trophies than books. Mr Dunwoodie had been a notable amateur boxer in his day. It had an outlook which Alice considered better than her father deserved, but tonight the heavy curtains were closed over the large window. He now beamed at her with a benevolence that had, prior to his incarceration, been noticeable by its absence. Privately, Alice could accept that through her teens she must have been the very prototype of the proverbial pain in the backside, but she was not inclined towards apology. There had been faults on both sides.

'Well now,' he said. 'How's married life

suiting you?'

That, in Alice's view, was none of his damn business, although married life was in fact suiting her very well. She and Justin had achieved a perfect partnership as companions, in his business and in the marital bed. She said, 'Very well, thank you,' repressively.

'You've both been keeping your hands clean?'

In the literal sense Alice's husband, being an engraver, had great difficulty keeping his hands clean, but she knew that that was not what her father meant. 'We've both been staying strictly on the straight and narrow,' she said, not quite truthfully. Her first venture into crime had produced some unpredictable complications and ended for her in near disaster, but Alice had perforce discovered in herself a talent for forward planning and organization. In conditions of great secrecy, even from her husband, she had later assisted her former associates with the planning of a successful jewel robbery. But that, she was determined, would be her last venture outwith the law. The arrival of her infant son Hugh, now resting in his carrycot under the eye of his fond grandmother, had presented the dangers in a new light.

Her father decided to ignore any lack of warmth in his daughter's reply. 'That's good. There's a little matter that I want to discuss with you. I'm still on probation, so I have to be very careful.'

The nerve of it almost took Alice's breath away. Almost but not quite. The two regarded each other in silence for some moments. Mr Dunwoodie was a heavily built man. His eyebrows were shaggy, perhaps in compensation by nature for the thinning of his hair. He had a full-lipped mouth under a decidedly Roman nose. Alice decided that the blotchy colour in his cheeks and nose was more noticeable than before because prison had stolen away his former tan, leaving in its place an unbecoming pallor. All the same, Alice had noticed that he still moved with the grace of the physically fit. Alice herself was blessed with dark curls and a figure which men, Justin included, seemed to find to their taste.

'Now look here,' she said sternly. 'I'm grateful to you for leaving me off the hook and insisting that I was an innocent bystander. It was a far, far better thing that you did then—'

He waved a hand in airy dismissal. 'I hadn't a hope in hell of getting away with it,'

9

he said. 'There was nothing to be gained by dragging you in with me.'

'Or you'd have done just that?'

'That is not what I was going to say.' He sighed. 'The sad thing is that you had your caper going and I had mine – a much bigger one – and neither of us knew about the other's. So when our paths crossed, tragedy was inevitable. Your robbery of the supermarket strongroom also netted my store of Euro forgeries. Even then, if we'd spoken to each other we could have saved a whole lot of trouble and expense. One of life's great ironies. If each of us had known that the other was stepping outside the law we could have worked together...'

He was stealing the initiative again. Alice grabbed for its coat tails. 'Grateful as I am, I've learned my lesson. And so has Justin. What's more, Justin had the fright of his life. He engraved the Euro plates for you and nearly landed himself in the muck along with us.'

'But for which you two might never have met.'

'We had already known each other,' Alice pointed out. 'Justin says that we're to stay inside the law and neither of us to take such a risk ever, ever again. And he's quite right.

I have no intention of putting my freedom, our marriage and your grandson's future at risk by taking any more chances. The business is picking up steadily. Anything we want that we don't have now will come to us if we wait patiently and honestly and work for it.'

'Unfortunately,' said her father, 'I am not in your happy position.'

'When you were rumbled, I asked how Mum would manage. You led me to believe that you had enough put by.'

Her father sighed and cast up his eyes. Alice guessed that he was about to make a plea for sympathy. His major asset, she reminded herself, had always been his ability to carry conviction. 'That was then. This is now. The lawyers pulled a bigger con on me than I ever managed to dream up. They told me that they could get me a reduced sentence if I appealed and, like a fool, I believed them.' His placidly paternal expression suffered a change and she glimpsed again the unforgiving despot of her schooldays. 'They did not get me a reduction of twenty minutes and they charged me the bloody earth. And now, of course, my legitimate earnings are down to nil. Who wants a financial adviser who's done time for setting up a counterfeit-Euro scam?'

'It's tough at the top,' Alice admitted. If she was touched by the anger in his tone or the pathos in his words, she was not going to admit it. 'If you're looking to Justin to engrave you another set of plates, put it out of your mind. He got badly beaten up and he could easily have gone inside with you.'

Her father met her eye. Something was amusing him. 'Suppose I could convince you that there's no way that anything could ever be traced back to us? One really good tickle and we could all decamp to somewhere warm and live the life of gentry. Let me tell you about it.'

Alice took a sip of her wine and settled back in her chair. 'You can tell me about it,' she said. She was being rash, she knew, but she was in the mood for a good after-dinner story. And after all the stick she had taken from her father during the years when he was pontificating about moral rectitude and pulling her weight in society while he was paying her school fees from the profits of one scam after another, she would take a certain pleasure in turning him down flat and reading him a lecture. Turns of phrase that could be guaranteed to make him foam at the mouth began to turn themselves over in her mind. He had thrown stones from his glass house for too long. Now somebody was going to throw them back.

Mr Dunwoodie took a folded paper from his pocket but he laid it on the table unopened. 'Did I tell you about Gus Castle?' he asked.

'You mentioned that you were sharing a – er – accommodation with him. No more than that.'

'A cell. You can say the word aloud. Yes. Right up to this morning, in fact. I think you might have liked Gus. You seem to have a soft spot for loveable rogues. You might even have trusted him, but you'd have been sorry. They let him out on day release for a few days to arrange and attend a funeral. He took the opportunity to access his e-mail. There wasn't a whole lot. Most of his contacts knew that he was inside. But there was one very interesting item.' Mr Dunwoodie paused for a moment's thought. 'You know, of course, that some Scottish castles, mostly clan castles, aren't known as Such-and-Such Castle but as Castle So-and-So. Like Castle Fraser.'

'And Castle Stuart and Castle Urquhart,' Alice said helpfully.

'Castle Grant and Castle Gordon and, don't forget, Castle Angus. But the English and Americans don't always know that. An e-mail had just been sent to Anguscastle – all one word – which is Gus's e-mail address. It invites the business manager at the castle to quote for a major wedding, estimated eight hundred guests to be put up for two nights in the castle or hotels round about, with meals including wedding banquet. Dates to be agreed, but the last week in August is suggested. Transport from and back to Aberdeen or Dundee Airports to be discussed. The enquiry is to be deemed confidential or all deals are off. Gus was due back inside, so he only had time to send an acknowledgement promising attention in the near future.'

Alice's curiosity rather than her interest was aroused. There had been several weddings of major celebrities in Scottish castles. 'Who signed it?' she asked.

'It's signed Juliana Hogwood.'

'Ah.' Alice was hugely disinterested in popular music but during a recent visit to the dentist there had been no reading matter in the waiting room on any other subject; and the name Juliana Hogwood would not have been easy to forget. 'She's the manager, agent and general dogsbody to Mona Lisa, the singer and pop star,' she said. 'I heard a

14

whisper that Mona Lisa was going to marry Craig Arthur, the American film actor. They denied it, so it's probably true. I suppose she feels that she has to keep up with Madonna and Paul McCartney. If so, why would they want to keep it secret? I'd have thought they'd squeeze maximum mileage out of the publicity.'

Mr Dunwoodie nodded thoughtfully. 'I have no doubt that they will, but it will have more impact if it bursts suddenly on the media. And they'll want to be sure that no fans or scandal-hunters or unauthorized mediaprats have a chance to gatecrash by lining up jobs as waiters or whatever.'

'That makes sense.' Caution suggested that Alice should back away and keep on going but curiosity spurred her forward. 'Between them, those two must have all the money in the world. What exactly did you have in mind?'

Her father laughed self-deprecatingly. 'I don't know that I had anything specific in mind. But, as you say, those two together must be almost a match for Bill Gates. Somebody said that Paul McCartney, when he had his showbiz wedding in another castle, must have spent two million. Good Champagne for eight hundred guests would set them back fifty thousand or more. The castle management might well plead a cash-flow problem and ask for money up front. You follow?'

'I'm ahead of you,' Alice said.

She was about to add that she intended to shoot so far ahead that she would be out of sight but her father was speaking again. 'I'm not a product of the electronic age,' he said. 'To me, a computer is only a super-type-writer which can also send and receive messages. If I want to make money disappear I do it the old-fashioned way by telephone or with portable assets. So I turn to you. I understand that it is possible to send e-mails that can never be traced back to the sender? Is that right?'

Alice was of a generation that learned computer hacking in the classroom. 'Well, yes,' she said. 'If what you're after is a short course in e-mail trickery, I can put you on to somebody. Given a laptop computer and a mobile phone, neither of which can be traced to you and both of which you're pre-pared to scrap when you've finished, you can send untraceable e-mails. Or you can route the messages through somebody else's mainframe and delete them afterwards, but that's getting a bit complicated.'

'Let's keep it simple by all means. What I was thinking, in my simple way, was that we could reply as from Castle Angus, giving quotes, arranging bookings and asking for deposits or cash in advance. If we get rumbled, we settle for what we've got up to that point, if anything, and close down; but if they really want to keep it confidential until the bitter end I don't see why we couldn't cut ourselves a piece of the wedding cake – at least right up until the arrival of the guests.'

On the point of explaining to her father that she was now a respectable wife and mother and that she had no intention of ever again stepping across the boundaries of the law and good behaviour, Alice was struck by the beauty of a vision. She kept a straight face, because even a smile would have shown weakness. The best sort of laughter, she thought, is secret laughter, because it does not have to be diluted by being shared.

She saw Castle Angus basking peacefully in late August sunshine. Into that placid scene suddenly intruded the bride and her groom. Alice knew Mona Lisa only as a figure occasionally glimpsed by accident on the TV screen – a singer with a style somewhere between Shirley Bassey and Tina

Turner. A singer of songs which were erotic to the point, sometimes, of being subtly lewd, although Alice had a vague recollection that she had been known to undertake more serious roles on occasions. Above all an entertainer, who presented herself as every man's fantasy sex object. Craig Arthur, if he was really her intended mate, was a competent actor whose charm was almost matched by his good looks and who had made a career out of a succession of highly successful films in most of which he, or a stunt man on his behalf, had survived some extraordinary dangers and subsequently at least once simulated the sex act, very convincingly, with one or another of the most beautiful women of the age.

So here would be this couple, happy until the very moment, these two who had only impinged on the edge of Alice's consciousness as having, infuriatingly, made huge fortunes by doing nothing that could by any stretch of the imagination be considered useful. On that basis, they were far more deserving of her father's disapproval than Alice had ever been.

These two, then, would arrive. And nobody would be expecting them.

The guests would be on their way and it

would be too late to intercept them. Singers of pop and rock and country and western. Comedians who lived by double takes, catchphrases, mimicking the accents of their guests and cocking an eye at the TV camera. Personalities without personalities. The famous who were famous for being famous and who therefore considered themselves to be above all normal rules of behaviour. All the people, in fact, whom Alice had come to dislike most in the world would be arriving at the door or at airports, surrounded by their personal bodyguards and sycophants, with no wedding to attend, no Champagne to drink, no accommodation waiting for them. They would mill around in disarray, lost and uncertain. Tempers would fray and behaviour would deteriorate, all under the eyes and lenses of the world's media. That image was much more appealing than any prospect of money. The singer would expect to get hitched but the hitching would develop the hitch to end all hitches.

'Hold on a minute,' she said. 'Let's think what we're going to need. We want a different laptop computer.'

'You've got a laptop,' her father protested.

'And there's no way I'm going to use it for this sort of carry-on. We'll need to use the

19

same e-mail address as the original e-mail. Did you get his password off him?'

'I'm not altogether an idiot,' said Mr Dunwoodie.

Such was Alice's euphoria at the picture in her mind that she refrained from reminding him which of them had been incarcerated.

Two

Alice awoke late but Justin, who had returned through the night on a late, late train, was later still. Justin, sleeping, with his hair in disarray and stubble on his chin, always looked vulnerable and thus especially adorable to Alice. She left him to sleep in and she and Hugh were washed, dressed and breakfasted before he came downstairs in his pyjamas, yawning.

The Dennisons lived in a small, cosy house in an unimportant street of similar houses, bright in summer with flowers in the small front gardens. The house was semi-detached, about a century old, built solidly of stone and pitch pine and roofed with slates. Generations of occupants had left their marks on the house, sometimes improving but also adding both scars and character. The previous owner had been an elderly pauper who had neglected the place. Justin and Alice were working hard in the hope of bringing it back to good condition without spoiling any of its charm. The kitchen was bright with new fitments and fresh decoration. Alice had already selected the tiles for the floor and elsewhere. The work would be done as soon as funds permitted. But even before the room was in its final form it had begun to collect the clutter that distinguishes a home from a mere house. Painting and papering were in hand through the rest of the house but a new bathroom was high on the list of priorities. The old cast-iron bath had been repainted by hand, there was no shower and the WC cistern was so high as to be almost inaccessible on the many occasions when the ballcock jammed.

Alice brooded for a moment over her baby. Carrying him in her body, bearing him and then holding him had been a series of life-changing experiences but the ultimate result had been quite the most beautiful and well-behaved baby in the world. She left Hugh blowing happy bubbles in his basket while she looked after her husband. Justin usually took no more than cereal and toast, but he had not been well fed during his travels and had burnt a lot of calories during the night when Alice welcomed him to bed. She put two eggs and some bacon into the pan and set about slicing mushrooms.

'How was the trip?' she asked.

He yawned. He was usually quite present-able in a slim and intellectual style, but slowly wakening from an exhausted sleep he still looked dishevelled. His hair, however, which usually reflected his mood, was now lying flat, so it could be presumed that the trip had been successful. 'The travelling was endless,' he said. 'Maybe I should fly, but it only takes the pilot to get hiccups and your timetable goes to hell. At least you can read comfortably on a train.' He showed her the smile that always did something strange to her innards. 'The maker wanted the impos-sible at a budget price and in a hurry, but that's about par for the course and the client was more reasonable. We came to an agree-ment in the end. I'll give you the letter of instruction for the files. How was the family wingding?'

Alice had already decided to make no mention of e-mails. She loved her husband dearly but she felt that, on the subject of behaviour and the law, he was inclined to err on the stuffy side. Justin's own brush with the law had shaken his world to its foundations. In Alice's view the whole truth and nothing but the truth belonged, if any-

23

where, in a court of law and would be an unnecessary amplification of the marriage vows. 'Much as you'd expect,' she said. 'I repeated your apologies, which didn't fool anybody. I didn't really blame you. It isn't much fun, sitting through the in jokes of other families. Not that there were a lot of jokes. The occasion, as you can imagine, was inhibited by more than the usual number of topics to be avoided.' She put his plate in front of him. 'I'm going out now. I'll tell Colin that you'll be about – what? – say an hour, and I'll open the mail. After that I have some errands to do.'

'Fair enough,' Justin said with his mouth full. 'Do I come home for lunch?'

'I may have my hands full. Have lunch at the Copper Kettle and we'll join you if we can. May I take the car?'

'I suppose so,' Justin said. Her enquiry had only been a matter of courtesy. Justin's workshop was within walking distance and he rarely had business in the town.

It was early summer. Trees were in leaf and the small front gardens were again bright with lovingly tended flowers but Alice had no time, for once, to stop and admire the prospect. When Hugh had received attention, with Humph, Justin's golden retriever, on a lead, she struggled with the pushchair across two kerbs and they made the obligatory visit to the small park across the street. Humph disappeared into the bushes and returned after a few minutes, looking pleased with himself.

Justin's business premises were only one street away, but it was a newer and broader street of small businesses and inexpensive flats. Tucked into the ground floor of a looming block, there was a very small shop where sporting trophies and various gifts suitable for engraving could be purchased. Beside this was an office where there was a desk, a computer with its printer and a filing cabinet that also supported the essential kettle. Behind was a severe but well-lit workshop where Justin had his own bench and where Colin, Justin's assistant, engraved trophies, wedding rings and retirement presentation watches and Dave, the apprentice, carried out odd jobs and practised on pieces of scrap metal. Justin thought that Dave might be good some day.

While Colin cooed over the baby and Dave made a fuss of Humph, Alice opened the mail and disposed of the junk. One letter concerning design details she left for Justin's perusal. The invoices and accounts she put on the desk to deal with in her own time.

Humph was content to be left in the workshop, knowing that he would be cosseted with titbits. Alice pushed the pushchair outside again and along the street to a not dissimilar shop where computer hardware such as cables and keyboards occupied much of the window and the remainder was filled with placards advertising more expensive goods. Alice manoeuvred the pushchair up the two steps and in through the door against its strong spring. The shop was busy with posters and pamphlets and was stocked, like the window, with the less expensive minutiae of computing; but computers themselves seemed to be in short supply.

Dick McAllistair (more often known as Dicky after a famous Tricky Dicky) was alone in the shop. He was noticeably thin even to his lank, ginger hair through which a pale pink scalp could be seen. He was in a permanent state of nerves, though just what he was afraid of could only be surmised. Alice had first encountered him while she was attempting a course in business management. She had failed to graduate from the course, largely because of a refusal to study while her contemporaries were enjoying such nightlife as the town had to offer, but she had remembered enough of its material to stand her in good stead while running Justin's business for him.

Dicky had sailed through the course and, being already the stereotypical computer nerd, had set up for himself in electronic retailing. Alice regularly obtained goods and services from him for the business. He was competent enough to repair a faulty disk drive or update an antivirus program, but she counted her change, never let him take her credit card out of her sight and then checked any credit-card slips with care. She would not have trusted him as far as she could spit. His manner and his reputation were against him. Any lack of probity, however, would in this instance be advantageous.

'I want a laptop, cheap,' Alice said. 'Second-hand would be fine. A trade-in?'

'You hae a laptop,' he pointed out. 'You got a virus or something? If it's giving you trouble, bring it in and I'll sort it.' His voice was thick with the local variant of the Scottish tongue.

'I want another one that nobody knows about. Not even you, Dicky, ten minutes after the deal.'

27

'Ah.' Dicky, who had tensed up when Alice entered the shop, had begun to relax. At the hint that the deal smacked of roguery, he unwound. 'I hae een here,' pointing down on to the countertop. 'I was going to break it for the bits but you can have it for fifty. Nice model, nearly new. Only you didn't get it from me.'

That almost certainly meant that it had been stolen. 'Show me,' she said.

From under the counter, after a cautious look at the door, Dicky produced a smart black laptop by Sony. He began to reel off figures of speed and capacity but Alice did not listen. He would have told her that it could cook a three-course meal if that happened to suit his book and, anyway, she was unlikely to fill a thousandth part of its memory. She could see that it would meet her needs. 'What software's loaded?' she asked.

'A'most naethin'. I've been wiping it.' He looked at her through half-closed eyes, guile and curiosity competing for his expression. 'If you need any special help...'

'I'll remember you. How could I forget? I'll take the laptop, if you load a good Word program and throw in a telephone modem and a battery charger.'

Dicky protested that she was ruining him. Alice somehow managed to drag a mention of the police into the discussion. They settled eventually at sixty-five pounds. 'Right,' Alice said. 'I'll pick it up this afternoon. Have it ready.' She turned the pushchair. 'Hold the door for me. And understand one thing. You forget this transaction completely or I'll hire somebody to pull you out into the street through your letter box.'

She glanced back and saw that he was contemplating the letter slot in his shop door.

Alice's agreement with her father had been that, while he would lay out most of what little money was needed for the initial speculation, she would provide the laptop PC. Thanks to the hard bargain that she had driven with Dicky McAllistair Alice thought that she was getting the best of the deal, especially considering that, if the idea proved to be a non-starter, she would still have the PC to sell. She still had some of the supermarket's money. She called at the hole in the wall, deposited two cheques to the business account and made a withdrawal from her own current account.

By the time she approached home again,

she had been to the newsagent to pay for the papers and collect a magazine, visited her favourite supermarket (not the one where she had participated in the robbery) and bought socks for Justin in a multiple store. She cast a wishful glance at Justin's car, but Hugh was making hungry noises and she suspected that he was overdue for a change of nappies. When she was inside, the breakfast dishes were looking at her and she was only too aware that no beds had been made. Oh well! No doubt even the Great Train Robbers had had to attend to the mundane chores. She set to in a rush.

An hour later, she loaded Hugh, now asleep in his carrycot, into the car along with a large bag of infant paraphernalia. Humph went into the back. The beds were still unmade and such trivia as the hoovering would have to wait for another day. Her other duties were done, although she was beginning to doubt whether marriage and motherhood were really compatible with a career in crime.

The house where Alice had been brought up and where she had lived until Justin entered her life had the same comfortable and friendly air as the house which she now shared with Justin and yet it was subtly different – larger and in a more desirable street, with bigger gardens which were better if not always so lovingly tended. With Humph back on his lead, she carried the bag and the carrycot as far as the front door. She still had her key but as a courtesy she rang the bell.

Mr Dunwoodie opened the door to her and relieved her of the bag. 'Come away in,' he said. 'Your mother's out on some charity do.'

In one way this was a relief but, 'I was rather hoping to scrounge some lunch,' Alice said. She put the carrycot down in the hall, from where a cry would be heard almost anywhere in the house, and sent Humph out to join Suzy, the family Labrador, in the back garden under the lilac trees. The two were old friends and although each had left puppyhood far behind they roused themselves for a token play-fight before settling down to doze companionably together.

'There's plenty in the fridge,' Mr Dunwoodie said. 'I was just wondering what to do for myself. You can make something for both of us.'

Alice bit back a sarcastic retort and went into the kitchen – twice the size of her own, a difference which still rankled. They sat down to a cheese and mushroom omelette with salad. Alice accepted a small share of her father's can of lager.

'I found a second-hand laptop,' she said. 'I'll collect it shortly. It won't be traceable to us. How did you get on?'

'I drove to Dundee and back, just to be safe, and paid cash for a mobile phone and enough phonecards to keep it going until Christmas.' He opened a box and transferred the mobile phone to the table. Alice was pleased to see that it was a different size, colour and shape from her own mobile, so there was no room for confusion there. 'They promised me that it would be online this afternoon,' Mr Dunwoodie resumed. 'I gave Gus's name and his home address, because that's where the authorities will make a start when the shit hits the fan, to use the vernacular.' He paused and looked doubtfully at his daughter. It seemed that their partnership in a less than legal activity had at last convinced him that she was sufficiently grown up to be exposed to bad language. 'I took a post office box in the same name. Gus will be all right. He has the original perfect alibi.'

'We don't want to deal by correspondence,' Alice pointed out. 'That would mean leaving all sorts of physical evidence.'

'I know that,' her father said patiently. 'I was doing this sort of thing before you were born. But when it comes to opening bank accounts they're going to want an address to send statements to.'

'Good thinking,' Alice said pacifically. When she had washed the dishes they settled in the study. Alice borrowed a pencil and paper. 'We mustn't wait too long or they'll try some other castle, if they aren't already getting competitive quotes,' she said. 'Let's draft what we want to send. I suggest something like this: "The last week in August is clear at present. Please select date, specify which areas of castle you would wish to use and what services you wish this office to arrange. Costings will then follow." How does that sound?'

'How do we sign it?'

'Pluck a name out of the air,' Alice said. 'Or sign it as Mrs Silver. As soon as they make direct contact with the castle, the game's up anyway. You'd better go and visit the castle, collect brochures, take photographs and try to get some kind of idea what sort of figures would sound credible.'

Her father looked alarmed. He was firmly seated but he managed to give the impression of backing away. 'Not me,' he said. 'They're bound to have security video cameras all over the place and if the con comes off they'll be looking through the tapes to see who visited. For God's sake! I'm only just out of the pokey. Can't you do it?'

'I have a husband and a baby,' Alice reminded him. 'I can't just buzz off for half a day or more without any convincing explanation. Justin would go up in smoke if he realized what I was up to. He only got away with engraving those plates for you by the skin of his teeth. His hair stood on end for a fortnight, which meant that he had the fright of his life. Now that he's a father he's thinking of adopting "Respectability" as an extra middle name.'

'He'll damn soon notice when you start spending the money.'

'He knows that I have something left from the first caper. After all, he was in on it. He just doesn't know how much and he doesn't want to know. He's closed his mind to the past.'

'A good trick if you can pull it off,' said Mr Dunwoodie. 'Your mother is much the same. Even when I was in prison she managed to convince herself that it was a miscarriage of justice. We're probably going to need another partner to do the running around.' *And take the rap if it goes wrong* was unspoken. 'What about your friend, the one who went abroad. Didn't I hear that she's back?'

'Sarah.' Alice considered. Her friend Sarah McLeod had begun her career in crime alongside Alice, but when that first adventure had slipped from failure towards disaster she had thrown in her lot with the two men who had been their accomplices. Together the three had pulled off a series of robberies and Sarah had shared rather more than a professional relationship with each of the men. The three had retired to the Costa del Crime and seemed set to live happily ever after but, as Alice had heard the sad story, the two men had overspent their shares and had been caught trying to rob a security van in Gibraltar.

Sarah's image had appeared on a number of security videos. Alice had even recognized her on *Crimewatch*, but only because she had known Sarah for years and was watching for her. Sarah had a talent for disguise and could have made a career in acting if she had been prepared to undergo the privations of the apprentice years.

'Yes,' Alice said. 'Sarah could do it. I'll

phone her as soon as that mobile's hooked up.' She paused and listened. 'Hugh's still sleeping. Keep an ear open, an eye on him and a pair of hands ready to pick him up if he starts squealing. I'll go and collect that laptop.'

Hugh was still asleep when his mother returned. The laptop was opened on Mr Dunwoodie's desk and Alice set it to booting up. The battery was freshly charged. Lines scrolled up as the inbuilt programs loaded. Suddenly she put out a hand and stopped it. 'The original purchase was registered to a Mr McSatan. Could there really be such a name?'

Her father chuckled contentedly. 'Of course not. That was one of the names Jock Brora used when he was setting himself up as a hard man in Glasgow. You've heard of him?'

'I've heard the name,' Alice said, 'but not in any favourable context. Who is he?'

'He controls a small gang which goes in for hijacks and intimidation, but he has his finger in innumerable pies. Always quick to spot a business opportunity is Jock. It must have been stolen from him. Or else he sold it. Or would he have traded it in for something bigger and better?'

Alice shook her head. 'Stolen, definitely, or why would it turn up here at a bargain basement price?'

'You're right. Well, this could be to our advantage. When we've finished, we let this fall into police hands and Jock will be lumbered with it.'

'You don't sound too concerned for him. What happened to honour among thieves?'

'That lasts until the first time that one party or the other pulls a fast one. Then it's every thief for himself. Jock Brora short-changed me in a deal over some fake etchings once. When I tried to collect, he threatened to set his heavies on me. I blacked his eye for him and knocked two of his teeth out,' Mr Dunwoodie said with satisfaction. 'I can be hard too, when it's called for.'

Alice knew that he had worked out regularly at a local gymnasium but she had difficulty imagining her father, who had always maintained an outward image of gentlemanly probity, rough-housing. She decided to avoid what could prove a touchy subject. 'I think I'd rather back the car over it and drop it into a skip,' she said. 'Less chance of a slip-up. Let's get that message ready. I've been thinking it over. I suggest we add something like this. "During the current recession our suppliers as well as ourselves are experiencing problems with cash flow. We will be able to offer better terms if goods and outside services are paid for in advance and deposits are put down against castle services." How does that come across?'

Mr Dunwoodie slapped the desk. 'Admirable! I knew that you were the right partner for me.'

'So did I. Let's see if the cellphone's functioning yet.'

They devoted some time to polishing the draft e-mail and by then the phone was connected.

'We'll need a bank account,' Alice said.

'We'll need several, for dumping the money in and moving it around.'

'We need one soon. Internet time will have to be paid for by direct debit.'

'Leave it with me. Come back tomorrow morning and we'll send off our reply.'

Alice made the first call on the new phone. Sarah was available and sounded pleased at the contact. They arranged to meet. By then, Alice could hear the sound of Hugh stirring in the carrycot so she gave herself an hour's grace.

'I expect you heard all that,' she told her father. 'You'll have to keep the phone and the laptop here. You have the luxury of a study all to yourself. There's nowhere I could keep them in my small house without Justin finding them or hearing the mobile if it rings.'

Her father thought and then nodded. 'I suppose that's fair.'

Alice dealt faithfully with Hugh on her mother's kitchen table and then allowed her father a few minutes to socialize with his grandson. Mr Dunwoodie came with her to the door. While they were saying their farewells in an atmosphere of mutual satisfaction, Mrs Dunwoodie's Audi turned into the drive.

Alice's mother was a plump lady, soft and gentle in mind and body. She could never believe ill of her family even when the evidence was incontrovertible and as a result her family, while pursuing their own lives inside and outside the law, were careful to protect her from any consequences. She was loud in her sorrow that she was getting only a passing glimpse of her grandson.

'I'm coming back tomorrow to pay Dad another visit,' Alice said. 'You can take Hugh for a walk then, all to yourself.'

Mrs Dunwoodie expressed her delight. 'I'm so glad that you're getting on better with your father,' she said. 'I hated it when you used to rub each other up the wrong way.'

'We seem to be getting on like a house on fire,' Alice said.

Mrs Dunwoodie sighed happily. 'We're a family again,' she said.

Three

The Dunwoodie home backed on to a golf course. This formed another source of envy to Alice because, despite the risk of being stunned by a sliced drive or exposed to bad language as its consequence, golf courses, being scenic and relatively immune to development, are desirable neighbours. The Dennisons' own back garden abutted on the similar plot belonging to a family with children so wild that all attempts at cultivation had been abandoned. A tall hedge kept out most of the flying toys but none of the noise.

For meetings of special confidentiality, when those participating would very much prefer to avoid any likelihood of their encounter being noted and remembered, Alice had occasionally used the shelter beside one of the tees. In her experience, the few midweek golfers were too concerned about the rough and bunkers ahead of them to notice or remember the faces of casual dog and baby-walkers. There was a path direct from her parents' back gate, but this was too uneven to make the passage of a pushchair anything other than hard labour. She drove to the clubhouse car park. Wheeling Hugh in his pushchair and with Humph on his lead, she followed a narrow but smooth path that undulated through the roughs. Sarah was already seated in the shelter. She was a young woman of Alice's age, fair haired and with a round face and dimples. Her eyes were large and yet it was her full mouth which gave expression to her character and her frequent changes of mood. She had a good figure but managed to stay slim in spite of a healthy appetite for good food.

Alice left Humph and the baby beside Sarah and went to look carefully behind the shelter in case somebody should be within earshot, perhaps relieving himself against the back wall. All was well. She decided not to bother again. The dry gorse would make a silent approach impossible.

Alice and Sarah had met twice for coffee or a drink since the latter's return home but only in the company of others, so there had been no opportunity to chat about their earlier adventures. Alice was not in the mood for idle chatter. She came quickly to the point. 'I didn't like to ask,' she said, 'but I don't think you're exactly rich any more. So would you welcome the chance to put something away in your piggy bank?'

'I've just bought a sports car,' Sarah said. 'So I'm nothing like as well heeled as I was two days ago and I wasn't exactly rolling then.'

A few minutes were taken up in a eulogy of Sarah's new MG. Then Alice said, 'Dad and I are getting together on something new. If it comes off it should be a good earner and, either way, it's as safe as anything ever was. Dad and I are taking one share each and he's promised the originator a half-share. If you want to come in as a general gopher, you can have another half-share. That's just under seventeen per cent, in case your arithmetic isn't up to it. As far as we can see, we won't need anybody else. Are you interested?'

'I'm interested,' Sarah said. The corners of her mouth were down-turned, a sure sign that she was unhappy. 'But first you'd better tell me what's got up your nose. We were friends for a long time but since I came back you've avoided me. I thought you were off me altogether until I got your phone call. Now, just for the sake of discussion you understand, I'm also interested to know why I only rate half an equal share. Is that for the same reason and if so what?'

An all-male foursome was playing through. The golfers spared the two young women an appreciative glance and one of them looked admiringly at Humph, but the presence of a baby was an effective turn-off. Alice waited, enjoying the view between mature trees and over shaven grass until the tee shots had been played and the men hiked off along the fairway.

'Then I'll tell you,' she said when the golfers were beyond earshot. 'First, because you didn't get in on the ground floor. But second, and more important, because after we split up you came back to me and—' Alice paused and listened but there was no rustling in the gorse – 'and I planned your big one for you. It came off smooth as silk but I only got a small part of what I'd been promised. That's why. You owe me.'

Sarah flushed and looked away. The two had been friends since their schooldays and she found that being made to feel guilty was more than ordinarily hurtful. She had rather hoped that Alice had forgotten about the money or was sufficiently euphoric in her new life not to care. 'You did get your share of what had been fenced up to when we left for Spain,' she said. She could hear in her own voice the whining note which echoed an occasion when she had let Alice's hamster escape down the back of the settee. 'I kept reminding Tod and Foxy and they kept putting me off. I don't know whether they ever fenced it or not. They were spending money as fast as we realized it. And then the two idiots tried to pull off a job on their own and got jugged in Gibraltar and I didn't dare go near them, so God alone knows where the rest of the money or the jewellery is, if there was any left. It wasn't my fault.'

'It may not have been your fault but it was your responsibility,' Alice said severely. 'You should have insisted that they treat me as a secured creditor. I'd have settled for a carefully chosen selection from the more nondescript items – a diamond tiara or something. Anyway, this is a biggy, it's as safe as they come and it doesn't even call for much effort. Do you want in or don't you?'

'Tell me about it,' Sarah said. 'You know that I won't spread it around, either way.'

Alice listened again and then began the tale. Sarah, who, like Alice, had outgrown her early reverence for those who had been catapulted to fame and fortune by luck rather than talent, was immediately captivated by the concept.

'I have a baby and a husband who mustn't know anything about it,' Alice explained. 'So I can't go dashing all over the country and Dad is too recently out of the pokey to show his face where it might be remembered. You're the Girl with a Thousand Faces. We need somebody to visit Castle Angus, collect brochures, take photographs and try to get an idea of what charges we should suggest. You do have a camera?'

'I have a damn good camera. That's another reason why I was just thinking about looking for a rich husband or another partner in crime.'

'There you are, then. It'll make a nice run for the new car. Your parents won't get suspicious?'

'No way. They think I was living with a Spanish nobleman but came home because I've decided to mend my ways. Well, there's no law against taking a look,' Sarah said. She looked at her watch. 'Too late now. I'll go tomorrow morning.'

Alice nodded. 'I'll have to fly. I have a house still upside down and a husband who'll expect a meal on the table in about an hour and a half. Come to Dad's house tomorrow as soon as you get back but don't march in with a band playing. Call me on my mobile first.'

Alice fled home. Several years earlier she had failed her business management course, but one of the lecturers had expounded the mysteries of the Critical Path Network and she had recognized it as no more than a rationalization of how she arranged her time anyway. Applying its principles now, she managed to make the beds, tidy the house, change Hugh again (just one damp thing after another, she told herself), take the laundry out of the tumble-drier and still have a meal almost ready for the table by the time Justin arrived home.

The nursery was a small room under the sloping roof. The agreement had been that Alice would do any interior painting requir- ed and Justin would attend to the papering. The door and other woodwork were now shining white but although the wallpaper, complete with clowns and animals, had been purchased it remained rolled up in the cardboard box. At the present rate of pro- gress, Alice said, it would be hung in time for little Hugh's entry into secondary school, to which Justin had replied that some later child might get the benefit. Alice, who was in two minds about further pro-creation, refrained from comment.

Justin found her kneeling beside the cot, soothing Hugh to sleep, and he smiled at the picture of the perfect wife, comfortably domesticated and happy in her little nest. He brought upstairs to her a rather dilute gin and tonic and they kissed deeply and contentedly, all as usual. He had washed but he still smelt faintly of polishing oils. 'How was your day?' he asked.

'Run off my feet,' she said with perfect truth. 'How was yours?'

He smiled again, tolerantly, as she knew that he would. Justin held the usual mascu-line belief that any well-organized woman could run a house, do the shopping, care for a family and cook meals in the course of an hour or so, leaving the rest of the day free for socializing. 'I've drafted a couple of letters and left them on the keyboard,' he said, 'and there are one or two accounts to send out and bills to pay.'

'I'll deal with them in the morning.'

Hugh had settled into the sudden and pro-found sleep of the very young. Justin pulled Alice gently to her feet and out of the nursery. Alice found that the potatoes, so often critical to the timing of the meal, had reached perfection. As she sat down, Justin was pouring wine from their only decanter. The fact that the wine had come from a box was tacitly ignored. They had two sets of wedding-present wine glasses and Alice noticed that Justin was pouring into a pair from the more capacious set.

'Are we celebrating something?' she asked absently.

'I'm in a mood for a minor extravagance,' he said. 'I made a start to Mona Lisa's lock-plates today and they're going really well.'

In her surprise, Alice nearly poured gravy into her wine glass. 'Who?'

'You know who I'm talking about. Didn't I tell you? The singer. She's the client I went to meet at Cogswell's the other day. Keep it under your hat but she's getting married soon, all very hush-hush. I don't know who the lucky man is. She wasn't at all what I expected.'

Alice judged it better not to reveal any prior knowledge. 'What did you expect?' she asked.

Justin put down his knife and sipped his wine while he reflected. 'I suppose I expected somebody like her usual on-screen image, half-dressed, very loud and very sexy,

49

with a mass of red hair. One tends to forget that she sometimes appears in the Proms and in Gilbert and Sullivan. In fact, I didn't recognize her at first. She's smaller than she looks on the box, quite petite and very ladylike in a tweedy sort of way and she must wear a wig on stage because her hair's brown and quite short. But her nose is bigger than they make it look. They must do something clever with the make-up and lighting.'

'What was she wearing?'

Justin gestured vaguely with his fork, surprised by the question. In his view, women were either clothed or not. There were subtle variations between the workaday and the dressed-up-to-the-nines, but the details were unimportant. 'Something countryish,' he said at last. 'Expensive. Tweedy, like I said, but very soft tweed.'

'Jewellery?'

'I didn't notice?' (Alice cast up her eyes at this.) 'She's giving her fiancé a top-of-the-range gun as a wedding present and buying a twenty-bore for herself and she wants both guns engraved with game scenes. She must be spending the earth and then a bit. She could buy a superlative car for the money, but the guns will be there long after the car

50

would have gone to the crusher. She seemed quite happy with what I sketched for her. But they're buying an estate in Perthshire and she seemed more interested in talking about cover crops, partridges and the Euston system and how to train a spaniel.'

It seemed that there was a proper sort of person behind the screen image. For the first time, Alice developed qualms about spoiling this paragon's wedding day. 'You'd be able to talk to her, then.'

Justin nodded. He had been brought up on a shooting estate. 'We got along fine. She's invited me to their first shoot in October.' He chuckled. 'I think she was coming on to me.'

Alice's newborn picture of Mona Lisa as a respectable and platonic playmate for Justin and a valued client to the business vanished. In its place came a half-remembered picture from the TV screen of the singer, in clothes so revealing that on any other woman they would have been taken for underwear, leering suggestively. In this vision, the singer had an exceptionally large nose.

Alice had no intention of giving Justin up to a large-nosed, underdressed singer or anyone else. In her view a woman who lost her man to another woman was not really trying. She always tried but it seemed that a little extra effort was due. Justin soon responded to her first hints and by gentle stages through the evening she brought him to the simmer. But she did not let him boil over until she herself was good and ready. She had read all the right books.

Justin was usually an early riser and, in a burst of enthusiasm for the fresh outlet for his talents, he was up and about next morning while the birds outside were still stretching and scratching. This suited Alice very well. The rather bland tenor of her usual days often left her mind restless and even after love-making she needed a calming topic to help her to sleep. She had lulled herself to slumber by planning in her head a major wedding for two international personalities and, with the event clear-cut in her mind, was looking forward to the start of another busy day.

She saw Justin off to work, only to meet up with him an hour and a half later when, leaving the house in reasonable order, she brought Hugh and Humph round to the workshop. She was required to spend a few minutes expressing admiration for Justin's designs for the engraving of the new lockplates before she was free to attack the mail, messages and accounts, but this came easily because, in his field, Justin really was an artist. His wildlife scenes were carefully composed within scrolled borders and she knew that when the designs were miniaturized and reproduced they would be faithful to or even improve on the originals.

When all was in order she told Justin, 'I'm off. I need the car again.'

Justin did not even look up from his work with the lining tool and graving hammer. 'That's all right. I shan't be going anywhere.'

'Perhaps it's time I had my own car,' Alice suggested.

This time, Justin did look up. 'We couldn't afford much of a second car yet.'

'I might be able to afford one myself.' This was an understatement. Alice could well have afforded a new medium-priced car or an upmarket second-hander.

Justin frowned, indicating with a flick of his eyes his two employees. 'I don't like you dipping into your own money,' he said. His eyes said 'ill-gotten gains'.

'Well, just as long as you don't mind me monopolizing our car...'

With the priorities established, Alice hurried home. Humph had to have his run in the park. Remembering how often her mother was out on charitable business, Alice tossed a mental coin to decide whether she would prefer to take lunch at her parents' expense while faced with the assumption on her father's part that, being junior in age and gender, any kitchen duties fell naturally to her. She decided to lunch at home. If they were equal partners, let her father get his own lunch. She rushed through some over-due hoovering, fed and changed Hugh and was attacking a plate of cold meat and salad when her mobile phone played its little tune. Sarah was calling to say that she was on the way back. Discretion suggested that that was quite enough discussion over the airwaves.

Hugh, thankfully, had fallen asleep. Alice was becoming highly expert at loading the car with all the necessities. She drove to her parents' house, dead-heating with her mother. She delivered Hugh to his delighted grandmother and sent Humph to join his pal in the garden.

Mr Dunwoodie welcomed his daughter into his study and they settled down. The desk held a stack of *Yellow Pages*. 'Sarah's on the way back,' Alice said.

Her father acknowledged the information with a nod. 'I've laid out some money, but

I'll get most of it back if we abort. I've opened half a dozen bank accounts over the cellphone, all with different banks. The principal one is in the name of Gordon Construction and I transferred five hundred into it. That one in particular gets shut down in a hurry when we've finished with it. The others are in names suggesting building trades, to make it reasonable for payments to be made from Gordon Construction. I set up a bill-paying facility, listing each of them and transferring a small sum each time. We'll probably open and close a dozen more before we've finished.'

While he spoke, Alice was booting up the laptop computer and plugging it together with the mobile phone. She brought AOL online and downloaded their software. As soon as she fed in the Angus Castle identity an incoming e-mail repeated the earlier message and demanded a prompt reply.

Alice hesitated for only a moment while her mother's upbringing warred with her father's genes. She was not concerned, indeed she was delighted, at the prospect of embarrassing a group against whom she felt a sour resentment at their being so rewarded for such dubious talents. She found not for the first time, that her worlds were divided in two. The world circumscribed by convention and the law was gently illuminated by her love for Justin and Hugh and by her contentment with the growth of their business and the progress of their house towards the perfect home. She enjoyed her walks with Humph and her outings with Justin; and she revelled in the miracle of love-making. But in some lights that confined world had the lustre of a suet pudding. It was the other world outside the law that drew her towards its siren light, not for the acquisition of goods or purchasing power but for the raw excitement of straying beyond the permitted line. Even the risk was no more than an added sparkle. Her father, she knew, felt the same.

Her hesitation passed. She reached the decision that had been inevitable all along. The ready drafted e-mail, with a few words of apology added for the delay, went off in the name of Angus Castle. Alice signed it *Castle Management Services.*

'Well, now we're committed.'

'We could still abort,' Alice said, but she mentioned it only as a matter of academic interest. If she still had reservations about ripping off an individual who had now developed a degree of reality to her, any suggestion that the singer had flirted with Justin went a long way towards overcoming her qualms.

'That's true.' Mr Dunwoodie looked at the clock on his desk. 'Shouldn't your friend be here by now?'

'She was going to call at one of those prints-while-you-wait places to get her film developed.'

'Do you trust her?'

'At least as much as I trust anybody else,' Alice said. 'Present company possibly but not necessarily excepted. You'll find that she's pretty good. She uses her brain. And not just her brain. One of her advantages is that if we need some information that can only be got by pillow talk, she's your girl.'

'A bit of a tart?' Mr Dunwoodie suggested.

Alice thought about Sarah. She had never really considered her friend before. Sarah just was. 'No, she's not a tart. As far as I know, she's never looked for a gift of any kind. I wouldn't even call her promiscuous, not quite. She just likes men, loves sex and doesn't have any hang-ups about it. And she seems to fancy the older man rather, which puts you in with a chance.' She watched her father as she spoke. If introducing him to Sarah proved to be an unfortunate move she owed it to her mother to drop a spanner in the works.

But Mr Dunwoodie combined a dismissive gesture with a grunt signifying disapproval. He seemed to be on the point of saying that that was not the sort of suggestion that a girl should make to her father, even a father who had only emerged from prison on the previous day, but Alice noticed that he sat up a little straighter and raised his chin. 'I hope she knows how to keep her mouth shut,' he said.

'She knows how,' Alice said. 'When she opens it, she doesn't give any more away than she wants to.'

A few minutes later their discussion was interrupted by the sound of the doorbell. Alice had heard her mother wheel Hugh away in the direction of the park. 'I'll go,' she said.

On the doorstep, she found a respectable-looking lady with fair hair touched by grey. She was wearing a smart business suit and carrying a briefcase. 'I've come about your insurance.' The accent was faintly Edinburgh.

Although she was expecting her, it took Alice several seconds to be sure that this really was Sarah. Out of the corner of her eye, Alice could see Mrs Dundee, the compulsively curious neighbour, pause in midweed. 'My father's expecting you,' Alice said distinctly. 'Please come in.'

Mr Dunwoodie got up to greet the guest. 'We've met before,' he said, 'but you're older than I remembered.'

Alice laughed. She had seen Sarah at work before. 'Sarah and I are the same age to within a few weeks,' she said. 'Next time you meet her she may be a teenager. Or a crone. She's good at voices and it's amazing what a touch of make-up and a slight tint to the hair can do.'

Sarah gathered from this that she was, for the moment, forgiven and she shot Alice a look of gratitude. 'And paper hankies in my shoes to change my walk,' she said. She accepted the more comfortable of the visitor's chairs and kicked off her shoes. Humph, who had insinuated himself back into the house and who knew Sarah of old, settled down with his chin on her feet. 'On the other hand, Mr Dunwoodie, you haven't changed a bit.'

Mr Dunwoodie looked pleased, but he only said, 'So how did you get on?'

'I had to pay six quid to get in,' Sarah said. 'Even then, some of the principal rooms weren't open to the public because there was some kind of a conference going on – North Sea exploration, I gathered. They didn't want to let me in at first, but there was a coach-load of Japanese who had made a booking. They were being given a tightly conducted tour and I just tagged along. I collected some brochures that show photographs of the bits I couldn't get into. There was a notice up saying not to take photos but I ignored it and nobody said boo to me at first. The Japanese were snapping away like fury.'

There was a pause while Sarah opened her briefcase and laid out the brochures and her many photographs. 'The interiors are a bit dark,' Sarah said, 'but they were for information rather than pictures and I didn't want to draw attention by using a flash. I had a fast film in the camera, so you can see as much as you need to see.'

Among the numerous photographs of imposing interiors and formal gardens surrounding a palatial construction of dark stone were several of obvious difference. Mr Dunwoodie isolated them. 'What are these?'

Alice craned her neck.

Sarah's manner became defensive. 'Now here,' she said, 'I may have exceeded my

60

brief. I couldn't get into the dining room – or banqueting hall or whatever they call it – because lunch had already been prepared for the delegates, but there was a menu and seating plan in the entrance hall and also plans of the castle. I decided that these would probably give you more of the information you wanted than anything else. The hall was in the newer part of the castle, a huge, echoing space and not very well lit so I had to use my flash. The next thing I knew, somebody was breathing down my neck and asking, very politely, what I was up to.'

'And you got tossed out on your ear?' Alice suggested.

'By no means and far otherwise.' Sarah smiled complacently. 'Who's telling this? I found that I was confronted by a really nice old boy, in his late forties or early fifties, I'd say, but with a good head of hair. Corduroys and a sweater with a hole in it. From his voice I put him down as Eton and Oxford, but he could have been anybody from an off-duty butler to a poor relation of His Lordship. I only had a few seconds to decide whether to be an ignorant foreigner or an illiterate day tripper. And this is where I may have overstepped the mark, but within the first few seconds I knew that he rather fancied me and that we could get along like that.' Sarah held up two crossed fingers. Alice winked at her father. 'So I put on a rather sexy voice and said that it was very hush-hush at present but that I was representing a film star who wanted to remain nameless for the moment but might be interested in arranging a really super-dooper wedding at the castle and did they by any chance have any kind of a tariff or price list?'

Mr Dunwoodie drew breath sharply. Sarah looked unrepentant. 'I know,' she said. 'I know. But, like I said, I only had a few seconds to make up my mind. Anyway, I haven't exposed anybody except myself and if the balloon goes up in a month or more they won't even be able to give an accurate description of me.

'I said that it was too confidential for names at this stage but that he could call me Sally. He said to call him Tom. He took me through into an office with more than one desk, but there was only one woman working there. They fed me coffee and a heap of figures, all subject to knowing exactly what facilities were wanted. I said that I hoped to be back in touch and Tom said much the same except that he put a slight emphasis on the word *touch*. Old goat,' Sarah said indulgently. 'While I was waiting for my films to be processed I went for a bite of lunch and jotted down as much as I could remember.'

Before Mr Dunwoodie could cavil at a tenuous link having been established between the castle and himself, Alice jumped in. 'I think you've done very well,' she said. 'You've got just the sort of information we're going to need if we're not going to frighten them off by making some damn silly mistake. The way show business chit-chat gets exchanged, these people probably have a damn good idea how much it should cost. I'll take the photos and the laptop away and rough out a plan for the wedding. Meet me tomorrow morning, Sarah, elevenish on the golf course, and you can help me to put some figures against the parts. I suggest we ask for twenty per cent up front for castle services and full advance payment for supplies like Champagne.'

'You seem to be switching into your bossy mode,' her father told her. 'What did you have in mind for me?'

'You could use the mobile phone to find out things like how much per passenger-mile helicopter transport costs and the same for limos. And get a list of prices from your wine merchant.'

Mr Dunwoodie considered. 'I can't fault it,' he said at last. 'Go ahead and be bossy. It seems to suit you.'

'I'm only trying to think ahead,' Alice said. 'But there's one other thing. We don't want them phoning the castle because there was something they've only just thought of. We'd better suggest that any personal contact should be by way of the mobile phone and ask for Miss ... Miss McDenwood. That's a bit of each of our surnames, if you hadn't noticed. We can kill her off later.'

'Not one of your best ideas,' her father said. 'An investigating officer is just as capable of thinking of that as you are. What do weddings suggest? Venus. And wines? Vinous. Make it Miss Vines.'

Four

In order to prepare an excuse for immuring herself in the nursery for the evening, Alice had decided to tell Justin that Hugh was teething; but this minor lie proved unnecessary. Justin had put in a solid day's work on the engravings and felt like a little recreation. He proposed to go down to the social club for a pint and a game of snooker. Like the perfect husband which he usually aspired to be, he suggested that they invite one or other of the grandparents to come and sit in so that Alice, who enjoyed snooker without being particularly good at it, could come with him. Alice declined with thanks and settled down with the laptop and a paperback copy of *Planning Your Great Day*, purchased specially from W.H. Smith.

There was, it seemed, far more to the planning of a proper wedding than Alice had supposed. With the bride's father released from prison for the day, her own marriage to

Justin had been a small affair before the registrar with only immediate family present. She had attended one or two bigger affairs and had noticed the traditions observed and the hospitality provided without ever considering the work that the bride's family had had to undertake, but the paperback was an eye-opener. She set to with an enthusiasm boosted by imagining herself and Justin in the major roles.

When Sarah and Alice met next morning at the shelter beside the fourth tee, Alice was carrying a printout of a complete wedding plan, listing everything that she or the book's author could think of, from the bride's bouquet to the services of the toastmaster. They considered it together.

'The castle can sleep three hundred and eighty,' Sarah said. 'That leaves four hundred and twenty to be distributed around the hotels. I wonder what they do about attendants. I bet that most of the guests would want to bring their secretaries and their own dressers and hairdressers.'

'Or probably a huge entourage. Good point. Obviously for a big show-business wedding you couldn't provide ten times as many beds as guests. I think we'd better assume that guests would be told that secretarial and hairdressing services would be provided and that any guests who haven't yet learned to dress themselves would have to make their own hotel bookings for their nannies and mummies. Ditto for body-guards. Bedrooms in the castle would be restricted to those with no hangers-on or who were prepared to provide hotel or B & B accommodation for their helpers and probably pay for it as well. It makes a good question to put to the client. "Adding veri-similitude to an otherwise bald and uncon-vincing narrative." And all the hotel-dwellers to be transported to and fro.' Alice keyed in some figures and looked at them thought-fully. 'You skipped rather lightly over the great outdoors. Tell me again.'

'You can drive right up to the frontage of the castle,' Sarah said patiently. 'But there's a huge area walled around at the sides and back with informal gardens, lawns where I'm told that helicopters regularly land and take off and a vast terrace where guest cars and coaches can be brought in through a massive pair of gates. There are tennis courts and even a nine-hole golf course inside the wall. There are stables and horses, but they're outside.'

'I'll tell you what I'm thinking,' Alice said

67

slowly. 'From the seating plan, the dining room can seat four hundred. The long wall seems to be mostly big windows. If those open all the way, a marquee on the terrace could double the dining capacity. It's that or do it all by marquee, but then there might not be room for helicopters to land. What do you think?'

Sarah studied one of her own photographs. 'Your way would work,' she said. 'I like it. It gives a well-considered impression to the client.'

'Right. Now let's pencil your costs in. We'll aim to err on the high side. She won't be impressed by cheapness and she'll be aiming to let it be known that her wedding cost more than Madonna's.'

'Good point! What would you call that? One-up-personship?'

'Something of the sort,' Alice agreed. The two were slipping easily back into their old, flippant relationship. 'Or gamespersonship. And the more she spends the more she can get by selling exclusive rights to *Hello* or some such rag. Come to think of it, I bet that's why there's so much emphasis on confidentiality. I wonder if she picked Castle Angus because, the way you describe it, security would be easier than almost anywhere else. We'd better allow a good sum for security guards.' She looked at her watch. 'Nearly finished. I meet Dad in an hour and a half so let's get on.'

'He's an attractive man, your father.' Alice looked at her sharply and Sarah laughed. 'Don't worry, I never mess with a married man.'

Alice decided that a brief deferment of work would be acceptable in favour of a more interesting topic. She returned a guarded smile. 'What is this with you and older men?' she asked. 'Does the suggestion of money and power turn you on?'

Sarah looked surprised. 'Certainly not that. Half of them have lived long enough to spend any money they used to have.' She considered the question seriously during the arrival, slicing into the rough, and dejected departure of a male twosome. 'I've never really thought about it before,' she said. 'It just happens. I suppose ... Yes. I'll tell you what I think. I think I shy away from the younger man. A young stud goes mad for you. He knows exactly what he wants and he'll be the fountain of romantic gestures until he gets it. Then he's quite happy if you just lie back and think of Scotland. You think you're a participant but really you're a sex object, just a piece of meat providing the right amount of friction. Afterwards he's happy, but sooner or later, maybe a year or maybe only ten minutes, he'll say, "It's been great but..." An older man isn't so confident. Think for a moment. What gets you started?'

Alice thought about it. They sat in silence for a minute while Alice tried to imagine Justin saying 'It's been great but...' The picture refused to come. She turned her mind to Sarah's question and decided to answer honestly. 'What turns me on,' she said at last, 'is my man becoming excited. That's what I respond to.'

A mixed foursome had arrived and was waiting for the two men preceding them to hack their way out of the rough. Sarah lowered her voice. 'Exactly! But that happens instantly with your young stud. He wants it now and he doesn't give you time to appreciate the run-up. Your older man needs time. He needs reassurance. He needs to be coaxed and titillated. Perhaps it's because I'm patient and sympathetic, but it only takes me a few minutes to suss out what's going to turn him into a tiger. Then, if I'm careful, I can spend ages being the ultimate temptress and working the miracle. That's a turn-on if you like. And in the end he's just so grateful he's ready to build a temple to me. His afterglow lights up the whole world. And that makes me feel just as good. I've done somebody a good turn, just as they told us to in the Guides.'

'I don't think that it's quite what they meant,' Alice retorted. But what Sarah had said fitted so neatly into her own more limited experience that she almost began to look forward to the day when the ageing process might restrain Justin's impetuosity. 'So you're looking for a rich *old* husband?' she asked.

'I'm looking,' Sarah said thoughtfully. 'Come to think of it, he doesn't have to be old. Or rich. Or a husband. But I think I'm ready for a permanent relationship with somebody who wants a permanent relationship with me.' She sighed. 'I'm tired of one-night stands and short stopovers. I tell you this, Alice, I could make somebody a wonderful wife. I have a whole lot of fidelity bottled up inside me, bursting to get out.'

'Don't bottle it up for too long, it may go off,' Alice said. She decided that that was enough on the subject. 'By the way, we've decided to use the name Miss Vines over the cellphone unless you've any other ideas.'

Sarah frowned in thought. 'I used the name Sally when I visited the castle. Well, it's a legitimate contraction of Sarah. I was going to use the name McLure if I had to give a surname. It's near enough to McLeod to be passed off as a mishearing if push came to shove and anyway I don't want to be loud, I'd rather think of myself as a lure.'

'McLure let it be, if we ever have to quote a name for you. I'll tell Dad. Now, let's put a figure against flowers.'

Back at the Dunwoodie house and before joining her father in his study, Alice quickly checked that her mother had not neglected Hugh's health or comfort. All seemed to be in order. Mrs Dunwoodie was in the garden, watched by the anxious Humph while she wheeled a somnolent Hugh to and fro, beaming all over her face.

Alice had left the laptop on the desk on her way to the golf course. It was already logged-on. 'We have a reply,' her father told Alice. 'The twenty-second of August would suit them and they would like an immediate indication of costs.'

'That's just what they're about to receive and may the Lord or somebody make them truly thankful.' She called up her wedding plan and they began to insert the pencilled figures from the printout.

'Regarding wines,' Mr Dunwoodie said, laying a printed list on the desk, 'I presume that they want to supply their guests all through the wedding day plus the prior evening. I don't see them giving the guests the first drink and leaving them to pay for their own thereafter – that's the desperate resort of a man marrying off his fifth or sixth daughter. I suggest that we quote the prices of the wines I've underlined and let them decide what to order, cash up front. They can choose between sale-or-return and keeping any surplus to stock their new home.'

Alice cast her eye over the list and found the prices shocking. 'They're not really going to pay this much, are they?'

'I don't suppose they'll want cheaper Champagne than Dom Perignon. I've given them some choices to make in table wines and liqueurs, but if you want the best you have to pay for it. And if you want to impress your peers with great years and famous names, you pay for that too.'

They worked their way through the wedding plan. 'Regarding the wedding itself,' Mr Dunwoodie said, 'they can't expect us to do everything for them. They can make their own choice. Do they want it in the castle or the cathedral? The local registrar or an archbishop? We'd better put in a contingency sum for an organist. We can copy the menu that Sarah photographed and suggest a late lunch and a buffet supper, at five-star hotel prices. Will they want evening entertainment or will the guests provide it?'

'Ask them to make the decisions,' said Alice. 'What figure do you think we should put against bed and breakfast?'

A few more phone calls filled in some gaps. When they had carried the fiction as far as it would go, pending firm decisions from the happy couple, Alice turned the format into a tidy e-mail. 'How long a delay would they find credible?' she asked.

'Quick but impeccable denotes efficiency,' said her father. 'We'll send it this afternoon.'

Alice left her father to attend to the dispatch of the e-mail.

The period of stressful overload left her tuned to activity and she entered a period during which she rushed from pillar to post, attending to Hugh, walking Humph, overhauling the filing, correspondence and bookkeeping at Justin's business and embarking on some serious repainting in the hall and staircase at home. She largely forgot about Mona Lisa and her approaching nuptials except when some major extravagance had to be postponed for financial reasons or while soothing herself to sleep with a mental picture of her least favourite celebrities arriving into the melee at the castle. Once or twice she shook the bed with a sudden fit of giggles and had to improvise some amusing thought for Justin's benefit. Mr Dunwoodie, meantime, absented himself for most of each day and was understood to be giving overdue attention to the boat that he kept for fishing trips.

Every two or three days she was summoned by her father. Mr Dunwoodie could well have sustained the correspondence with Mona Lisa's staff but he was not a trained typist and his broader fingers found it difficult to single out a key without touching its neighbours. Even when Alice was at her busiest she responded cheerfully to his calls, because her mother was so pleased to have charge of Hugh for a while and was also delighted that Alice and her father had transcended the friction of Alice's rebellious years and seemed happy in each other's company. She was quite unaware that the new bond between father and daughter was the recently discovered common talent for criminal activity.

After a delay of several more days, which Alice put down to the huge cost of the proposals, another e-mail arrived. Alice hurried over in the evening to discuss it with her father. Somebody had considered their proposals point by point, approving or modifying and making choices from the options. Wines had been selected, in quantities which made even Mr Dunwoodie blink. There was no quibbling over the quoted prices. A 20 per cent deposit against castle services and hotel bookings was acceptable and prepayment would be made in full for wines and other purchases. An invoice and a preferred method of payment were requested. A booking would then be confirmed.

After the work that had gone before, the preparation of an invoice took only a few minutes. The sum due, running as it did well into six figures, was formidable and, once again, Alice would not have been surprised if the proposal had died the death; but after all, she assured herself, their outlay had been small. The account number and address for a money transfer was added and the reply despatched.

Another few days went by before her father again summoned Alice. This time, even Mr Dunwoodie seemed slightly stunned. The booking was confirmed and the sum due had been transferred to the Gordon Construction account. Total confidentiality was still a prime requirement.

Alice phoned Sarah, but Sarah had made no provision for receiving any such sum as her share. 'Keep it for me,' she said. 'I trust you. More than you can trust me, it seems.'

'Don't be silly,' Alice said. To her father she said, 'I feel much the same. Keep it safe for me and I'll draw on you when I need it. You'd better start covering our tracks.'

'Teach your granny to suck eggs, my girl,' said her father. 'I'm already shifting the money around between accounts. Do you want me to invest it for you?'

The question gave Alice cause for thought. It made no sense for the money to be lying around and attracting no interest while being eroded by inflation. Interest-bearing deposit accounts would be referred to the Inland Revenue. A few tax-free investments might meet the case without producing any fresh problems.

'Leave it for the moment,' she said. 'Let me think about it.'

As far as Alice was concerned, there the matter rested. They had pulled off a successful scam and the next they would hear of it would no doubt be in the media. They postponed dumping the laptop and the cellphone in case there might be further requirements from Mona Lisa resulting in more money transfers. The only problem giving Alice cause for concern was how she would explain her sudden wealth to Justin when the time came to take advantage of it. Not far from her parents' home, there was a substantial house which she had always coveted and there was talk of the old couple quitting it to move into the granny flat attached to the house belonging to one of their sons. The couple had always been friendlily disposed to Alice and she thought that they might be agreeable to selling their house, nominally, at a bargain-basement price and accepting the difference in the form of a secret payment. How good an idea did Justin have of current local housing prices? She would have to sound him out.

The partners in crime had conveyed almost too good an impression of building a better mousetrap. (And mousetrap, Alice thought, was the perfect metaphor in the circumstances.) E-mails continued to arrive. Somebody had given serious thought to transport and had arrived at credible estimates of the mileages entailed. Reservations were required for the helicopters and again for limousine service and for flowers. Each time, the 20 per cent deposit arrived promptly and was as promptly magicked away into a series of bank accounts which opened and closed like flowers in the sun. Alice and her father agreed that such largesse was too good to be spurned. Long might it continue.

It was, of course, too good to last.

Five

The first break in the placid rhythm of their days came two weeks later. Alice was in the office, carefully labelling several trophies that had come in for engraving. There had been an unfortunate incident earlier in the summer when Colin had engraved a large cup for a men's athletic event with the name of the Mrs Ethel Anderson who had triumphed in the showjumping at a gymkhana. The resultant uproar had only been calmed by the provision of a replacement cup at the firm's expense and its engraving with the 136 names of all the winners that had gone before – by Colin in his own time. Since then, no names were engraved until Alice had personally checked the name and its spelling and attached a label.

She was interrupted by the warning bell on the shop door. She looked up. A woman of slightly more than her own age entered. The new arrival was neither beautiful nor homely but she had a very good figure and lustrous eyes that Alice would have killed to possess. She was plainly dressed but there was no doubt that her clothes were expensive and well chosen. When she spoke, her voice was deep and well modulated but had a faint trace of an accent that Alice thought of as vaguely north of England.

'Have I come to the right place?' she asked doubtfully. 'This is where Justin Dennison produces his wonderful engravings?'

Alice warmed immediately. Appreciation of Justin's work was a sure way to her heart. 'It is. Can I help you?'

'I was expecting something more like an artist's studio in a film set. I should have known that life is never like that. I'm just on my way north. I'm planning a few days' break fishing the Aberdeenshire Dee. When I realized how close I'd pass to here, I thought I'd call in and see how he's getting on with my lockplates. He won't mind?'

'Of course not,' Alice said automatically. Her mind was swimming. The only two sets of lockplates in the workshop at the moment were Mona Lisa's, but surely this couldn't be the singer? In her mind, Alice dressed her visitor in skimpy stage clothing, made her up heavily (camouflaging the slight prominence of her nose) and fitted her with a wig resembling a mane of auburn hair and she realized that, yes, it very well could. The accent, she thought, might be faintly Liverpool although on stage the singer sounded mid-Atlantic. Her nose did not look particularly large, but perhaps that had been a fiction provided by Justin and intended to emphasize his disinterest. Was that, she wondered, cause for comfort or a danger signal?

'Will they be ready soon?' the singer asked. 'You see – can you keep a secret?'

Alice smiled in spite of herself. The girlishness of the question was disarming. 'If it's who you are and that you're getting married, my husband already swore me to secrecy. I look after the business side, so I was bound to know who was the client. Congratulations. I hope you'll be very happy.'

The visitor lit up – that was the only way that Alice could find to describe it. 'I know I will. And you didn't say a word? No, you couldn't or it would have been all over the tabloids by now. I'm getting married late in August and the twelve-bore's a wedding present for my fiancé. He's finishing a film just now and he starts another one in the middle of September when I have to go on tour, so we can just fit in a honeymoon going from one clay-pigeon competition to another around the States. That's his idea of heaven as long as I'm careful not to beat him. Can I see my lockplates?'

'Come this way. Don't get oil or grit on that lovely tweed.'

'Don't worry about it. Workshops are hell to keep clean, aren't they?'

The singer was delighted with the work, which was approaching completion. Justin promised to finish within another day or so. 'I'm making it bold,' he said. 'It won't be so conspicuous after the colour-hardening.'

'It seems a shame to cover it up.'

Justin matched the singer's grin. 'Next time you come this way, bring the guns in and I'll show you a few tricks for making the engraving stand out again.'

The singer spent a few minutes chatting with Dave and Colin, admiring Humph and crooning over Hugh. Alice could not detect the faintest trace of any sexual signals between Mona Lisa and Justin. The singer left behind her a rapt group of admirers. 'I'd prefer that you don't tell anybody about my visit,' she said as Alice escorted her to the door.

'She doesn't want us talking about her visit,' Alice reported. 'I wonder why not.'

'Because she doesn't want to have to go

around with a whole gaggle of minders,' Justin suggested. 'Like she is just now, who'd recognize her?'

'Damned if I would,' Alice said. 'If she hadn't asked to see her lockplates, I'd have asked her who she was and what she wanted.'

Alice had been made freshly aware that an enormous stumbling block had been placed in the singer's path to her Big Day. She had liked Mona Lisa. As a sop, she reminded herself of the host of celebrities whom she despised and who, she hoped, would bear the brunt of the inconvenience.

She consoled herself with the thought that every scam must have a loser and that Mona Lisa could well afford the loss of a few hundred thousand and could easily reschedule her wedding or enjoy the honeymoon without the sanctity of marriage. She put it out of her mind and concentrated on the business, the house and her little family – until, that is, she was interrupted in the preparation of a tax return by a phone call from her father. Mr Dunwoodie sounded seriously perturbed. His car would be waiting at the end of the road.

'I'm going out,' Alice said. 'Keep an eye on

Hugh?' Justin, crouched over his beading tool, grunted, but Alice could be reasonably sure that either Colin or Dave would see to it that Hugh was preserved from disaster. 'Everything you could need is in the bag,' she added.

Alice's mother had her own car, so Mr Dunwoodie's big Rover had been carefully laid up as soon as the tax disc ran out, for the duration of the period when he was unavailable to drive it. Alice found the car, shining and remarkably unworn for its age, parked in a bus lay-by just round the corner. Her father was in the driving seat and, as she approached, Alice saw that Sarah was seated in the back. Instead of being his usual smart and tidy self, Mr Dunwoodie was wearing jeans and an old shirt and sweater. The combination of circumstances seemed so unlikely that she almost stopped; but her father leaned across and pushed open the front passenger's door.

'What gives?' she asked as she pulled the door to. 'Exposing us with Sarah like this...'

Mr Dunwoodie set the car in motion. 'We have a crisis,' he said. 'I'll explain but I'll do it somewhere quiet away from home. I want to get out of the public eye and I don't want to think and talk and drive at the same time.

And I need a drink. Bear with me. As for being seen together, we've gone past that stage.'

Alice turned her head and met Sarah's eye. They shrugged in unison. Alice was reminded of the downside of criminal activity, the sudden sense of imminent disaster coming from an unknown direction. Five minutes brought them to the Cameron Arms, a comparatively new roadhouse but built to look old. At that hour it was predictably idle. A waitress tagged along as Mr Dunwoodie led them to a recess round a corner from the big and empty bar. The waitress looked for a moment as though she would refuse to serve Mr Dunwoodie in his paint-stained clothes and with the smell of fish about him, but she took a look at his expression and her courage failed her. Mr Dunwoodie ordered a double whisky. Sarah and Alice settled for tea.

'I've had a hell of a shock,' Mr Dunwoodie said. 'I'd better tell you and it comes easiest to give it to you in chronological order. I went to the boat. I wanted to touch up some scratches on the cabin-top and do a little fishing. The mackerel are running inshore at the moment. So one blessing is that at least I wasn't in a decent suit.

'When I got out ashore, they were waiting for me behind the bothy.' Mr Dunwoodie had a small cottage beside an isolated beach on the coast. It held some happy memories for Alice and her father and some much less happy and more recent memories for all three of them. It was there that Alice had been roughly handled, her father had suffered the arrest that had led to his incarceration and Alice had nearly suffered the same mishap.

'Who were waiting for you?' Alice asked.

'Two of Jock Brora's men. I don't know their names but I've seen them with him in the past. They had the whole story, with photographs of you, Sarah, at Castle Angus and the two of you together and copies of our e-mails. We've got a week to turn over all the money we've taken off Mona Lisa or Jock will give what they've got to the fuzz.'

'But none of that proves anything,' Sarah said.

'Agreed. But they showed me a laptop computer which looked very like the one we've been using. So the first thing I did was to go straight home and check and I found that the house had been broken into. Your mother was out, Alice, thank God, but now she's in a tizzy about a broken pane in the back door. Nothing was taken except that computer. It will have our fingerprints all over it and all that correspondence in its memory. Jock reported it stolen just about the time we acquired it. If they hand that to the fuzz when the news of the scam breaks, it'll connect up. A court might well convict. With my record it would be almost a certainty.'

'We could be out of the country with the money by then,' Sarah suggested.

'You could,' said Alice bitterly. 'I couldn't. I have a husband and a baby, in case you hadn't noticed, and Justin has a house and a business, which must be worth about as much as my share of the loot. I couldn't leave him to carry the can for the rest of us. And he'd never forgive me for getting us into such a mess anyway. How in hell did they manage to get on to us?' she finished angrily.

'I think I can tell you that,' said her father. 'Not that it helps. Before I left the house, I phoned each of you to meet me. I made one other phone call, to a man I knew in the pokey. He's one of those types with a finger in every pie and he owed me a big favour because I'd saved his bacon when a couple of hard men were laying for him. I let them know that if they laid a finger on him they'd have me to answer to. Believe it or not, I had quite a reputation in that place. He's out now, but before he got out he told me that if he could ever help me I'd only have to ask.

'He confirmed what I'd been guessing. Gus Castle used to be one of Jock Brora's minions and your friend Dick McAllistair in the computer shop has a connection with Jock Brora through his sister.'

'Jesus! The whole thing was a set-up?' said Sarah.

'Dead right! It started by chance when Gus got the e-mail, which was intended for Castle Angus. While he was out of the pokey on day release he spoke to Jock. Gus couldn't follow it up – for one thing he was due back inside that day and for another the e-mail address would lead straight to him. So they came up with the idea of letting us do all the work and take the risks. Gus gave me the e-mail and his e-mail address and password. That way, we could be counted on to do exactly what we've done and Jock could monitor our traffic without leaving any record to implicate him. He probably thought that he could take the money direct out of our bank accounts but I fooled him by using telephone banking instead of the Internet. Without the codes and passwords, he was stuck.'

'If we hand over the money—' Sarah began.

'Over my dead body,' Alice said.

'Mine too. But *if* we gave up the money, would that be an end to it?'

'I doubt it,' Mr Dunwoodie said. 'The only satisfaction I can get out of it is that I gave those two bastards something to remember me by. They were going to give me a hammering, just to ram the message home or perhaps for the fun of it. But hard men can go soft very quickly and then they depend on confidence and ruthlessness to make up for any lack of fitness. I was working out all the time I was banged up and I've forgotten more about rough-housing than those two ever knew. My ribs are sore, but those tossers will be walking bandy-legged for a month.'

The waitress returned with their drinks. The necessary silence was bridged with frantic thought. When they had privacy again, Sarah said, 'I still don't see what else we can do but run for it. I'm sorry, Alice.'

Mr Dunwoodie nodded. 'Stealing the computer was meant to give them a hold over us. But, in fact, it's also cut off one of our lines of retreat. We've lost all the information that was stored in it. If we had that...'

'But we do,' said Alice. 'One thing I've learned is never to count on a computer's memory. I've been had before by a crashed computer and I thought there might be follow-up queries, so I've been keeping copies on a floppy disk hidden under the lining paper in a drawer in my bedroom. I was going to burn the disk when we'd finished with it. I didn't tell you, Dad, because you were so uptight about leaving no back-trail. I don't see that it helps.'

'It helps,' Sarah said. 'Of course it does.'

Alice frowned. It seemed that, for once, her father and her friend were ahead of her. 'I don't get it,' she said.

'Yes you do,' Sarah said. 'Short of doing a quick runner, which would save us the money but leave the Dennison family with problems, we have two options. One, we give Mr Brora the money.'

'We'll go for Option Two,' Alice said.

'You don't know what it is yet.'

'I don't care what it is, I am not being blackmailed by a crook who set us up in the first place and then sent a couple of men to rough up my dad. What's Option Two?'

'We place the orders and go ahead with the wedding.'

Mr Dunwoodie nodded.

'I'll be damned and double damned,' Alice said slowly. 'So Jock Brora tells the police that we're committing a fraud. The police contact Mona Lisa and Castle Angus. And Castle Angus says, "Yes, of course, the wedding's all ordered. They've paid the deposits we asked for and just look at this mountain of Champagne." Brora ends up with egg on his face and probably charged with wasting police time. We get nothing out of it except a lot of hard work. Am I right?'

'We've already done most of the work,' Sarah pointed out. 'And we might still see a profit. In your own words, we decided to err on the high side when we were preparing our estimates.'

'Never mind all that.' Alice had thought that she would never smile again but now she could feel a big grin breaking out. 'I love it! I never cared that much about the money anyway and I was getting scruples about Mona Lisa. If I've got to choose between her getting the benefit of her own money or handing it over to a crook who sent men to try to beat up my father, Mona Lisa gets my vote.'

'Thank you for that display of filial affection,' Mr Dunwoodie said, but his tone was light. It was only when Alice saw that he had begun to relax that she realized how tense had been his body language. 'I regret the money, though, as Sarah said, we should still come out ahead of the game. We're agreed?' (Alice and Sarah both nodded.) 'We have a week before Jock plans to lower the boom. The first thing is to find out whether the castle is available from August twenty-first to the twenty-third inclusive.'

'And without using e-mail,' Alice said. 'No more e-mails using the Gus Castle address for the next week unless we want the enemy to see them.'

'Right. The first approach shouldn't be by telephone either,' her father said. 'A face-to-face enquiry followed immediately by a money transfer for a deposit. Then we've established our *bona fides* and we're in business.'

'What do we do if the castle can't give us August the twenty-second?' Sarah asked.

Mr Dunwoodie raised his hands in a helpless gesture. 'Then we're up the creek without a paddle. We ask Castle Angus what other dates are available and then ask Mona Lisa to choose one of them.'

'She won't,' Alice said. 'From what she told me, her dates are critical.'

'Then we find another castle and tell her that Castle Angus burnt down.'

'She'd soon find that it hadn't,' Alice pointed out.

'But by then we could have paid out for the wedding of her dreams and could hardly be had up for fraud. Oh, I don't know,' Mr Dunwoodie said impatiently. 'Let's solve the problems we have already, not the ones that may never arise. For the moment we have enough real ones to be getting on with. I suggest that we go to the castle, make a provisional booking and then arrange the transfer of cash. That should clear in a day or so. Meantime, we could be getting in firm quotations for the other goods and services. We'll have to set up a command centre.'

'It can't be at my house,' Alice said. 'I don't want Justin to know anything about this. What's more, I can't buzz off for half the day at a moment's notice. You'll have to go and talk to the castle with Sarah as your assistant while I clear my feet at the shop and make my peace with Justin.'

'Let Sarah go,' Mr Dunwoodie told Alice.

'All on my little lonesome?' Sarah said.

'They've already seen your face. You can explain that they misheard you and you're Sarah McLeod, not Sally McLure. I want to pack your mother off, Alice, just in case Brora tries to get at me through her. Your cousin Jane in Gourock, the widowed one, phoned the other night. She's having a baby soon, her third. She says that this one's a legacy from her late husband but I don't know, it's been a long time coming. She has two pre-school kids already. She was asking your mother to come through and help out and Mary's half inclined to go. I'll tell her that I'd be glad of the chance to go and get the boat fixed up and I'll put her on the train.'

'That means that your house would be available for our headquarters,' Alice said.

'Better not,' said her father thoughtfully. 'I think both those beggars are in hospital by now. If Jock has any more boys at his beck and call – which may or may not be the case – and if they come looking for me, that's where they'd look first. I was thinking of the cottage. We have four cellphones between us and you have a laptop so we can operate just as well from there. They wouldn't expect us to be back there and if they do come we can deal with them in decent seclusion.'

Alice nodded. There could be no doubt that the cottage or bothy would make an admirably private headquarters. She had no doubts about her father's ability to cope with any visitors. 'I'll tell Justin that you want my help with the boat. You usually do. Pick me up when you can.'

'I'll meet you there,' Sarah said.

Alice dismounted at the office intending, among other things, a furious assault on any outstanding paperwork so that her way would be clear to absent herself for a while. She felt as though a weight had been lifted off her. Instead of making a return into crime, she was about to make restitution to somebody whom she had genuinely liked and set up the wedding of the year, if not much longer. But when she entered the office she found Justin standing over the phone. 'Your pal McAllistair just phoned,' he said. 'He sounded excited. He wants you to get in touch.'

Alice could only make a wild guess as to why Tricky Dicky was getting excited, but the reason was unlikely to be connected with the business. A call from the shop phone with Justin listening might not be a good idea. 'I'll go round and see him,' she said. 'I wanted to query his last account anyway. And after that, my father wants some help with the boat. If Dad comes here before I'm back, tell him where to find me.'

'Right.' As usual, Justin was remarkably incurious outside of his work. When he surfaced at the end of the working day he might show more interest.

The street was unusually quiet. Alice felt a return of the hollowness inside her. She hated confrontations. She used her mobile phone to call her father. She had to wait for her call to be answered, but she knew that he would be looking for somewhere to stop the car. Mr Dunwoodie was not the slowest of drivers but he was almost compulsively careful in his driving and never answered his phone while the car was in motion. He came on the line at last. 'We may have another problem,' she told him. 'And I may need a big, strong man to protect little me. Join me at the Computerminus shop in Bridge Street.'

Her father wasted no time on words. He just said, 'I'll be there,' and disconnected.

Six

At the computer shop, she found Dicky McAllistair alone. He came out of the back room hastily, turned the sign on the glass door to read *Closed* and dropped the latch before retreating again behind the counter, leaning on it in a manner that was intended to appear negligent. It only looked, Alice thought, as though he was beginning to decompose. 'I ken something you don't know I know.'

Alice kept her voice level. 'I expect so. And I know a hell of a lot that you don't know.'

'I ken a' about your Castle Angus scam,' he said bluntly.

Alice found that her legs were shaking. There was a single bentwood chair for customers but she preferred not to allow him to look down on her from on high. She faced him over the counter. While she walked she had had time to figure out that this was at the root of his summons. She had also decided that until she had support she would defer any discussion of his demands – because demands would certainly follow. 'I suppose you were the spy who monitored our e-mails,' she said.

Tricky Dicky hesitated but vanity won the day. 'It was dead easy,' he sneered.

'It would be. You started off knowing the password we were using.'

Dicky waved this aside. He was clearly riding on a high. His voice was throaty with excitement. 'I ken tae the penny what you won out of it.'

'But you don't know where it is. I suppose,' Alice said, 'that it was you who kept Jock Brora informed about our movements?' Dicky nodded proudly, his Adam's apple bobbing. 'And you took the photographs?'

Dicky nodded again, almost preening himself. Alice noticed that his eyes glanced down to the counter. 'Jock gied me a camera. And what I want...'

Alice sighed. It seemed impossible to avoid the subject any longer, but her father should arrive soon. 'What do you want, then?'

He leaned across the counter and lowered his voice. Apparently Jock Brora threw a long shadow. 'If we come to an agreement, I could tell Jock that you'd paid out a whole lot more money up front or took in less than you did and I could back it wi' some copies of e-mails. How's about twenty grand? You hold that much out on him and we split it.'

'You're looking for ten thousand in your grubby fist?' Alice said incredulously.

'Aye, or I tell Jock just how much you did make. But listen. I can gie you a whale of a discount.' He leaned further over the counter until she thought that he would topple. As he muttered on, Alice, who had thought herself unshockable, was truly shocked by what he was suggesting. She had known that such practices existed without ever quite believing that they happened outside the fevered fantasies of perverts. Even the terminology was so unfamiliar that Dicky was forced, in a muffled voice, to interpret for her. Even so, his definitions lacked dictionary precision.

As an alternative to physical violence, Alice was still mentally formulating an expression of her abhorrence so all-consuming as to reduce Tricky Dicky to a small pile of smouldering ash when she saw to her relief that her father was at the door. She turned quickly and, before Dicky could prevent her or even utter an objection, she turned the latch and opened the door. Mr Dunwoodie, who had made his own guess as to the reason for Alice's summons, entered belligerently and Alice locked the door behind him. He seemed to fill the shop.

She spent an instant in wasted thought. She was slow to anger but now she was seething. It went against years of habit to use bad language to her father but on reflection there was no other way of expressing herself satisfactorily. 'This little shit,' she said firmly, 'did most of Jock Brora's dirty work for him and now he's prepared to diddle his boss out of twenty thousand and split it with us. Only he's offered us a big discount if I'll appear in a porn video. He wanted me to...' Alice's voice trailed away. 'I can't say any of it aloud,' she said at last. 'Make him tell you.'

Dicky McAllistair found himself leaning across the counter again, this time under the pull of a large hand which had taken hold of both his lapels.

'Just what did you want my daughter to do?' Mr Dunwoodie enquired in a low rumble.

'If you rough me up I'll tell Mr Brora.' This apparently was the direst threat the skinny youth could contemplate.

'If you want him to know that you were

preparing to rip him off for twenty grand,' Alice said, 'go right ahead. He'll love that. Tell my father what you wanted me to do.'

'Nothin' much.' Dicky's toes were barely touching the floor. His voice had gone up to a squeak which, added to the hoarseness caused by Mr Dunwoodie's grip on his clothing, made him difficult to understand.

'Tell him.'

'Och, you dinnae want—'

'Tell him. In the same words you used to me.'

It took time with several false starts but in the end Dicky McAllistair was forced to repeat what he had said to Alice. Mr Dunwoodie was properly incensed – he said afterwards that he had been so angry that he was seeing spots – and announced his intention of pulling the young man like a wishbone. He got so far as to invite his daughter to wish a wish.

This interlude had given Alice time to consider. 'What I wish,' she said sternly, 'is that you would stop beating your chest like a gorilla and think for a moment.' She paused, but once again more respectable language was surely inadequate. 'The last thing any of us want is to get the police involved, but if you damage this absolute arsehole – which I admit nobody ever deserved more – that's exactly what you'll do. Just keep him there for a moment without hurting him more than a little bit while I take a look around. And be sure that nobody comes to the door and sees you.'

She went through into the back room. This was primarily a workshop but there were high shelves holding packs of CDs and floppies, keyboards, speakers, computer games and other gadgetry. All that Alice was looking for was Tricky Dicky's Achilles heel. If spite overcame caution, as well it might, the idiot was capable of kicking up all sorts of stink. Alice hoped to spot some obviously stolen or otherwise illegal goods. None were immediately evident. But he had some sort of connection with the porn industry. If Dicky's stock was out on the shelves, what was the purpose of the large metal cupboard that stood against one wall? As she approached it, she realized that it was the source of a steady whispering sound. The doors were not locked. As she pulled them open, the sound increased.

The cupboard contained at least a dozen shelves and almost every shelf held a video recorder. To judge by the variety of makes and models, Alice judged that each had been stolen – VCRs, she knew, were a favourite target of thieves, being easily disposed of and almost untraceable. Every one was running in recording mode. It seemed that copies were being made from an original tape. It was a lash-up rather than a professional installation but it would do for small-scale and poor-quality reproduction.

There was a small television to act as a monitor, although its screen was blank. Alice found the ON switch and the screen came to life. In unnatural silence, two men were forcibly undressing a girl. Her vigorous resistance seemed to Alice to be feigned rather than genuine.

Alice returned to the front shop. Her father and Dicky McAllistair were much as she had left them, although the younger man's face was turning blue. Alice ignored the by play and made for the drawers under the counter, the direction in which Dicky had looked when the camera was mentioned. Sure enough, she found a large Polaroid camera.

'He's copying porn videos in the back room,' she told her father. 'Tidy him up a bit and bring him through. One moment.' Justin had a similar camera for recording the progress of work. She made sure that the camera had film and that the flash was working. Mr Dunwoodie thrust Dicky in front of the open cupboard and Alice took photographs. The action had moved on and the girl had now been reduced to panties and stockings. Her protests still looked like amateurish acting so Alice guessed that either the caning of her buttocks was being faked or the panties contained some secret padding. Dickie's expression of horror could well have been caused by the sudden intrusion of the photographer.

When she was satisfied that she had several incontrovertible photographs which included sharp images of the pictures on the monitor, Alice nodded to her father. He stepped forwards and removed one of the video cassettes. 'Listen,' Mr Dunwoodie said, 'I suggest that you keep your mouth tight shut. One word to anybody and the police get these prints and this cassette. Your workshop's easily recognizable. And you can't pass these off as glamour videos. This is S and M and you're a supplier. The police are having a crackdown just now. You'll have a rough time in prison, a pretty boy like you.'

Dicky was whimpering as father and daughter left the shop together. 'You think he's pretty?' Alice said.

Her father laughed grimly. 'I don't. But he probably does. And any headbanger in there for life probably would too.'

Alice visited the supermarket which she had once conspired to rob and stocked the freezer for several days. She made sure that Justin knew what food was in the house and how to cook it before kissing him fondly and promising to give him warning of her return home sufficient to allow him, or more probably young Dave on his behalf, to have the house clean and reasonably tidy. After that there was little to be done but to gather up her necessities and wait for her father to collect her.

As they loaded his car and put Humph in the back beside Suzy, Mr Dunwoodie said, 'Your mother went off quite happily. You women are strange. When she's at home she's in a hurry to go off on holiday to get away from cooking and cleaning – not that she has much cleaning to do with Bess coming in alternate days – but when she gets the chance to go where she'll have to do twice as much of everything and look after two bairns beside, she jumps at it. Why's that?'

'Same reason that I help you to paint your

beastly boat,' Alice said. 'Because it's so nice when it stops.'

'She wanted me to go to Gourock with her. I offered her an alternative. I suggested that if she was so desperate to get away from the house she could come fishing for a few days with me.'

The cottage – so-called – was an unofficial erection, which had somehow fallen between different legislative stools mainly because nobody who mattered knew that it was there. It stood on land owned by an absentee landlord and leased to a forestry organization which assumed that the cottage had been built with the landlord's permission. It was a suprisingly sound little dwelling, erected by members of the building trade who had owed Mr Dunwoodie substantial favours at the time, and it had been built using components from a cedar-boarded house which was in the process of demolition. It comprised a modest sitting-dining-kitchen, one bedroom and another compartment which contained a chemical toilet and a shower. It had been furnished with cast-outs from the Dunwoodie main residence. Some inspired finagling had resulted in mains electricity being brought in but there were no other mains services;

water came from a well and was pumped by electric motor into the roof tank; drainage was by soakaway. There was no gas and no telephone and drinking water was bottled or boiled. It was essentially a bachelor pad but Alice and Sarah had once managed to rough it there in some comfort along with two partners in crime.

Mr Dunwoodie nursed his Rover carefully over the track leading to the cottage. The track, which had originally been opened up by the foresters, was hemmed in between ranks of conifers. His care was as much for the baby on the back seat as for the car. He had argued at first when he realized that both Hugh and Humph were to be with the party, until Alice had pointed out that their presence was the price that she had to pay for being able to get away at all. He had admitted that the presence of an extra dog might give added security, but protested again at the small mountain of carrier bags that she had brought out. Alice was firm. Humph might need no more than his bed, dish, food, towel, brush and comb but her father's grandson was not going to be without anything pertaining to his sleep, toiletry, feeding, education or entertainment; and if that should necessitate attaching a trailer to the car or hiring a van, so be it. And she had had to do two lots of shopping; one for Justin and one for themselves. Mr Dunwoodie had subsided, grumbling.

'What kind of state is the place in?' Alice asked.

'It's all right. Friends of mine were using it while I was inside.'

'Oh. A slum, then. Were they hiding out?'

'Not a bit of it. I do have some respectable friends left. Fishing friends. Men stay loyal when somebody lands unlucky.'

That effectively silenced Alice, whose women friends had largely turned their backs since she made her appearance in court.

The trees fell back and, across an open area too sandy for trees, the cottage waited for them. The cedar boarding and shingles had weathered to silver and Alice had to admit that from outside it looked at least as neat and sound as when she had last seen it. From beyond a low sand dune came the eternal sound of the sea. As they approached the cottage, the boat came into view, nodding at its mooring buoy with a look of permanency. 'They had the use of it last year,' Mr Dunwoodie explained, 'so they painted and launched it for me this spring.'

The interior of the cottage had the smell typical of dwellings which have been shut up in summer weather, but that would soon blow away. Alice's fears were unfounded. The place was clean and tidy. Her father's friends must be of a higher calibre than her own associates had been.

While her father went to check on the boat's mooring, Alice sorted her priorities. Electricity on. Water pump on. Kettle on. Luggage in. Hugh clean, dry and fed. Both dogs fed and let out for a roam around. Bedding hung to air on the outside clothes-line. She arranged the three cellphones – hers, her father's and the one acquired specially for the scam – in a row beside the sink with her computer beside them. Then she stocked the cupboards and made a start to a meal for the adults.

Her father returned, confident that the work would mostly be done. 'Everything seems shipshape,' he said. Alice glared at him but before she could begin to express her total disinterest in his boat and her annoyance at having been left to deal with everything of even marginal importance unaided, their attention was caught by a little electronic tune. It came from one of the cellphones but it took them several seconds to identify which.

Sarah was on Alice's phone. 'I'm on the way to you,' she said. 'The twenty-second of August is clear and they've accepted the booking. I kept back Mona Lisa's name but I think they guessed. I negotiated rather better terms than they quoted last time. I said that we'd make a deposit of ten grand straight away. Is that OK?'

Mr Dunwoodie had put his ear close to Alice's. She raised her eyebrows at him. He nodded. 'That's fine,' Alice said.

'Better get that off now. Got a pencil and paper?' She dictated the bank account number and sort code. 'Now listen. They were a bit shattered when it dawned that there were only three and a half weeks to go, because the Mrs Silver who I met has gone to have her baby early and they have a new manager who doesn't know the job. I thought for a minute that they were going to turn us down. But they were keen to get the cash and publicity of a really big showbiz wedding and to keep upsides with the other castles and I said that we could make ourselves available to help with the organizing. That swung it. Tom said that, to judge from the detail we'd furnished already, we had to be on the ball. So as soon as the payment for the deposit clears they'll put an office and three bedrooms at our disposal. See you in about half an hour. And I'm hungry.'

'I could have betted on hunger, if nothing else,' Alice said. She disconnected. She considered offering her father a 'high five' but decided not to risk the embarrassment of discovering that he had no idea what to do about it. 'We're off the hook,' she said cheerfully. 'It's a curse, though, having to set to and do the work for real. I wouldn't know how to organize a top-of-the-range wedding? What happens if we blow it?'

'If we blow it, we're still in the clear unless she sues us for negligence or something. But you won't blow it. I thought women were born knowing all about weddings.'

'You thought wrong.'

'Come on, now,' Mr Dunwoodie said cajolingly. 'Any daughter of mine can turn her hand to anything.'

Despite their recent accord, Alice was not going to let him get away with that. 'You spent my entire teen years telling me how useless I was.'

'I'm sure I didn't.' Mr Dunwoodie hesitated and evidently decided that Alice was right. 'Well, we've all been to weddings. To judge by the lack of adverse criticism, you made a perfect job of it when it was only a paper exercise; now all you have to do is to turn it into a reality. And there are hundreds of publications on the subject. It's surely only a matter of common sense. Come on, now,' Mr Dunwoodie said cajolingly, 'what happened to the girl who organized the raid on the supermarket?'

'Don't even remind me,' Alice said. 'She very nearly followed you into the slammer.' She gave herself a mental shake. 'Let's get on with it then. What comes first?'

'I'll arrange that money transfer,' said Mr Dunwoodie. 'We'd better start getting competitive quotes for all the supplies. Check the e-mail again first. She may have quarrelled with what's-his-name and the wedding may be off.'

'I'll check,' Alice said. 'But, from the moony look that came over her when she said his name, there's more danger that she jumped the gun and they went to a registry office.'

'That would get us out of our difficulties,' her father pointed out. 'We could return the money and be bomb-proof.'

Mr Dunwoodie, to Alice's disgust, had brought a supply of old clothes and other gear suggesting that he hoped to indulge in a little sea fishing, leaving any real work to his female helpers, but she was pleased to note that he had had the forethought to bring the *Yellow Pages* for the Dundee and Aberdeen areas. When Sarah arrived, the meal was simmering gently; the deposit had been wired to the Castle Angus account and the Dunwoodies, father and daughter, were busily listing names, telephone numbers and e-mail addresses of suppliers, from wine merchants to florists and from helicopter operators to suppliers of tents and marquees.

Sarah had sounded cheerful on the phone but when she arrived at last she was moody. 'I'd forgotten how bad your track was,' she said, 'and I think it's got worse. I wish now that I'd bought a Land Rover. If I've done any damage to my MG it gets paid for out of the profits before share-out. I tried to drive with two wheels on the central hump but it only worked for some of the time. But never mind,' she added brightly. 'That smells good.'

'So it ought,' said Alice. She and her father marked the *Yellow Pages* where they were leaving off and transferred it to the draining board. While Alice laid the table and served the meal Mr Dunwoodie decanted wine. 'It may only be from a cardboard box,' he said, 'but it's quite respectable.'

'This is quite like old times,' Sarah said more cheerfully, looking round the wood-lined walls embellished with charts and other marine impedimenta, as they settled at the table. Alice noticed that Sarah had indefinably changed her hair and make-up. Her apparent age now lay somewhere between her real age and the more mature impression conveyed on her earlier visit to the castle. 'We had some jolly parties here,' Sarah added.

'Without my knowledge or approval,' said Mr Dunwoodie.

Alice was uncertain whether or not he was joking. She was tempted to point out that if he had been an honest man he would never have found out at all, but since there was considerable doubt as to whose fault had been the greater she decided to hold her tongue. Each party had been up to no good and quite unaware of the other's activities. Instead, she asked Sarah, 'How did you get on?'

'It began with a hiccup,' Sarah said. 'As I told you, Mrs Silver, the woman I met when I visited the castle last time, had left in a hurry to have her baby. It turns out that she was also going to get married for the second time, or possibly the third or fourth. There was a new manager, a Miss Evans, called in in a hurry. She didn't know anything about anything. There was a typist who can't do much but type and a local temp who helps out from time to time and nobody understood Mrs Silver's computer system. We'd have been at an impasse if old Tom hadn't been available. I still don't know what he does and he's a bit clueless about the fine details, but I sorted out the computer and after a hell of a lot of argument and more than a little name-dropping we managed to get Mrs Silver on the phone. She sounded a bit fraught, in fact I kept hearing a voice in the background telling somebody to push, but she filled in the gaps and between us we soon had the broad outline agreed.'

'Did you get a proper look at the place this time?' Alice asked.

They had to wait while Sarah, who had filled her mouth, emptied it. 'I did indeed,' she said at last. 'It's huge and my feet know all about it. I've got pages of notes and I can see exactly how a major wedding would fit into it.' She attacked her plate again.

When the meal was finished and the

washing-up completed – Mr Dunwoodie assisting under protest after being told firmly that this was a partnership all the way along the line – they sat down to finalize their lists.

'Take wine merchants now,' Mr Dunwoodie said. 'We don't want small local firms. The scale of this order should get the bigger firms interested. But we want them reputable, not fly-by-night.'

'We'll try the Internet,' Alice said. 'And go on noting e-mail addresses. We can send out a dozen e-mail enquiries in the morning, getting prices and delivery times for the Champagne alone. We'll use my e-mail address, not the Angus Castle one. Then we forget about anyone who's slow to answer and we get detailed prices and delivery dates from the best half dozen.'

'That sounds sensible,' said her father.

'When we get around to the marquee,' Sarah said, 'Tom told me that they've used that idea before. He gave me the name of the firm who erected it and told me their price. It's less than we'd allowed for it. And he gave me some names for helicopter and limo services.'

By the time they retired for the night – Sarah and Alice sharing the three-quarter bed as they had done in the past and Mr Dunwoodie on the airbed on the sitting-room floor – the list had been brought to a usable state. Sarah's last act before bed was to take a look outside. 'You're not afraid of somebody creeping up on us?' she asked.

'That's what the dogs are along for,' Mr Dunwoodie said. 'But I don't expect Jock Brora to get violent again. I duffed up two of his men, but they were laying for me. He'll have decided that his message had got through and he'll consider it a fair exchange. All Jock's after is the money and that wee squirt in the computer shop won't dare to report to him.'

Alice had finished her routine phone call to Justin. 'Don't be too sure of that,' she said. 'Tricky Dicky thinks that Jock Brora is God's personal fixer.'

Seven

It seemed that Alice was the more accomplished soothsayer. She was roused in the night by Humph's cold nose in her ear. Humph was notable for the strength of his bladder and never woke her except when he suspected something amiss. Alice put on shoes and a coat.

Her father was already up, roused in a similar manner by Suzy. He was looking cautiously through one of the windows. He sensed Alice's movement behind him. 'There's somebody out there,' he said. 'We haven't given Jock any reason to think that we're going to defy him, so he won't intend anything too drastic. I'd outwait him in here except that he may intend to teach me a lesson by torching my car or some such message. I'm going out.'

'Do be careful,' Alice said. As she spoke, she recognized the words as essentially feminine, unnecessary and probably infuriating, but it was too late to call them back. To make up, she said, 'Do you have a weapon?'

'I can manage. I'll take a stick. These are city loons. I'll be more used to the countryside at night than they are.'

Several stout walking sticks stood in the corner by the door for the sake of anyone walking along the beach. He was already wearing a grey coat. Grey is less visible than black on a dark night. He chose a stick by touch and slipped silently out of the door. Alice took his place at the window. It was not pitch dark outside but a high moon was screened by cloud so high that it looked nearer to the moon than to Earth. In the dim light Mr Dunwoodie's dark figure began to merge with the surroundings. Although her eyes were tuned to the darkness, Alice could only follow his movements because she knew where to look. When a movement drew her eyes to a darker figure beyond, she lost him. Her mouth was dry.

Just what emergency might arise, she had no idea. She could imagine dozens of possible disasters without having more than the vaguest idea as to what action her father would want her to take. She fumbled in the dark for another stick, choosing by touch the heaviest, and groped on the shelf for the lantern while hoping that it had been put on charge in the not too distant past. She returned to the window and picked out her father's silhouette in time to see him throw up his hands and fall. She heard him cry out although the sound of a shot had not reached her through the glass.

Alice forgot to wonder what her father would want her to do. The cautious part of her nature suggested that she stay where she was and let her father take his chances, but impulse took over. When she opened the door, the two dogs rushed out, barking. They might make a useful distraction but she was immediately afraid for them as much as for her father and far more than for herself. She followed more carefully, feeling with her feet. The night was warm despite the nearness to the North Sea.

Ten yards from the cottage, she stopped. Holding the torch out from her body – she had learned that much from the spy films on TV – she clicked it on. The light blazed across the ground and nobody took a shot at her. Her father was rolling on the ground, cursing like a fish porter and tangled in a net. Two men stood by, dumbfounded, while the dogs fawned around them.

Behind her the lights in the cottage came

on, adding to the brightness of the scene. The noise had aroused Sarah at last. 'What the *hell*?' Alice demanded.

'Rabbiters,' said her father wearily, beginning to pick himself up and shed tangles of net. 'Long-netters. Probably poachers.'

The nearer of the two strangers came to life. 'Poachers be buggered,' he said. 'We got permission from the Forestry to ferret and long-net here.'

Alice immediately felt wrong-footed. It seemed that the two men had the greater right to be there. 'Do you have to do it in the middle of the night?' she enquired testily.

'That's when you do it,' explained her father tiredly. 'It's the only possible time. Go back to bed. Our apologies, gentlemen. Next time, if there's a car at the door give us warning. Carry on.'

'Fat chance,' said one of the men. 'You've chased the mappies a mile awa and tied the net in knots.'

'So sorry,' said Mr Dunwoodie. He turned back towards the cottage.

The following day was devoted to phone calls and e-mails. The dogs and Hugh had to be satisfied with attention whenever other matters permitted. Most of the firms contacted needed time to check and work out prices, so by late afternoon they had run out of useful activity. They were sitting around the all-purpose table, checking over what they had already accomplished, and Mr Dunwoodie was taking a call on his cellphone when Alice, working one-handed because she was nursing Hugh in her other arm, visited the e-mail once more.

'There's a message from Mona Lisa,' she said in a hollow voice. 'There's to be a press release on Friday, in two days' time. Confidentiality will then be at an end.'

'We'd better get even more of a move on,' said Sarah. 'We can't have Castle Angus reading about themselves in the paper before we've completed the deal.'

'You're missing the point,' Alice said. 'This came in through the service provider we were using for correspondence with Mona Lisa. Jock Brora will have seen it.'

'Calm down,' said her father. 'You may have missed the real point. Think about it. From his point of view, this doesn't change anything. The fraud may be about to become public knowledge, but giving the police evidence that we're the guilty parties would still have the same effect. And that last call was from my friend, the one who owes me a debt for saving his skin. He picked up some more news. Jock Brora is getting desperate. He got involved in a really big drug deal which went sour. Now he owes far more than he can raise to some very hard dealers indeed who are more than ready to put out a contract on him. He needs all he can get and soon. We might be his only hope if we were a hope at all.'

'That's all very interesting and my heart bleeds for him, but if there are any points being missed,' said Alice, 'guess who's missing them. Mona Lisa makes a public announcement of her marriage and there isn't an immediate scream from Castle Angus to say that they never heard of it or her. Jock Brora knows that his plan has misfired.'

'And so he knows that he's already too late,' Mr Dunwoodie pointed out. 'But Sarah's right. We must tie up the deal with Castle Angus.'

Sarah picked up her cellphone. After a short call to Castle Angus she said, 'The money's in their account. Miss Evans just checked. So we're welcome to occupy rooms at the castle from tomorrow.'

'I must go home first,' Alice said.

'For a touch of the conjugals?' Sarah enquired.

124

'Not primarily. That would be a welcome spin-off. Let me think aloud. I'll need more clothes and supplies for Hugh. I want Mona Lisa's phone numbers so that we can give her the new e-mail address without Jock Brora being able to see what we're up to. I want to dazzle Justin with a better cover story so that he won't drive out here to see how we're getting on. Which of you is going to give me a lift home and pick me up in the morning?'

'Your dad will have to do it,' said Sarah. 'We could never squeeze you and your Humph and the baby and your mountain of food, supplies and spare parts into the MG.'

'In the morning,' Mr Dunwoodie said firmly. 'We have some more e-mailing to do first. Justin can wait that long.'

It may be that they had been lulled by the false alarm of the previous night. Or perhaps the interruption had left them sleepy. Whatever the reason, on the following night they were deeply asleep and were not easily roused when the dogs began snuffling and whimpering to warn of something different and possibly dangerous. Humph resorted to pulling the bedclothes off Alice.

She had a pocket torch beside the bed. She

dragged her eyes open and used it to look at her watch. It was just after two a.m. She put on a thin robe and saw that Sarah was doing the same. In the other room, the sitting- dining-kitchen, Mr Dunwoodie was silhouetted against the faint light of the window. At the sound of their footsteps he turned. 'Car coming,' he said. 'Still a bit off but the dogs could hear it.'

Alice immediately felt vulnerable. 'Jock Brora on the rampage?' she suggested.

'I doubt it,' said her father. 'If he decided on revenge, which I doubt, he'd be more likely to leave the car at the main road and pussyfoot up to the door, hoping to catch us at a disadvantage.'

'Who, then?' Sarah asked nervously.

'I don't know. But I doubt if it's a friend bearing gifts.'

'Do you have a gun?' Sarah asked.

'No. Get into a gunfight and if you win you're in dire trouble with the law and if you lose it you're dead. I prefer to rely on reason and intelligence. Last night was different and look where it got me. If reason and intelligence don't work, run like hell.' He switched on the single light and Alice saw that he was smiling. 'Better get some clothes on.'

He was right, Alice decided. Whatever was to come, dressed was best. In the bedroom, Sarah was already struggling into jeans over her pyjamas. Alice did the same. When they hurried back to the other room, the headlights of a car were sweeping the front of the cottage and there was no sign of Mr Dunwoodie. Outside, car doors closed. The sound of footsteps was almost inaudible on the sandy ground.

They arrived without immediate drama. The first was unmistakably the leader although the other was the larger of the two, physically formidable even without the blue-black revolver in his fist. The bigger man moved quickly to look in the bedroom and then the primitive bathroom. Emerging, he shook his head and then went to close the door and stand with his back against it.

The leader was as tall as his companion but he was lean while the other had the solidity of a pedigree bull; and he had no need of a firearm to compel attention. His hawk-like face, with high cheekbones and an arrogant nose, might have suited a Cambridge don, but his cold eyes fitted well with his air of absolute confidence. This man, Alice thought, had no self-doubts. He would go for his objective in the absolute certainty of attaining it. She felt a hollowness in her midriff.

When he spoke, there was a trace of an accent in which Alice detected both American and Spanish. Central American, she decided. His choice of words suggested a good but limited vocabulary of English. 'You had better sit down, young ladies,' he said. 'This may take a little time.' The words were polite but the tone was steel.

Sarah perched quickly on one of the kitchen-dining chairs. Alice, who had been about to sink into one of the easy chairs, decided that Sarah's was the sounder thinking. When they moved, they might want to move in a hurry. She hoped that her quivering knees would respond.

'There should be a man,' the leader said. 'The father of one of you. Where is he?'

Alice cleared her throat. Her mouth had gone dry. 'He had business to attend to,' she said. 'He went home for the night.'

'Leaving two pretty ladies on their own? That was unwise of him. Or maybe it was wise. We shall see. How much money have you collected for the unpleasant Mr Brora?'

'I don't understand,' said Sarah.

'I think that you do. However, so that we know what we are discussing, I will explain.

Mr Brora came up with the scam to get money up front from Mona Lisa towards her wedding. He let you think that you had ... thought of it first. Originated, yes? When you had collected what was to be had, he moved in and showed you that he could betray you to the police unless you handed over the money to him. I believe that he was going to allow you to keep a finder's fee of ten per cent.'

'He told you that?' Alice asked.

The man smiled thinly. 'After a little persuasion.'

'He didn't tell us.'

'Perhaps he intended to hold that much out. You see, Mr Brora owes my employers money. A great deal of money. He wanted Mona Lisa's money in order to pay off a substantial part of his debt, or so he says. We think that he intended rather to pocket the money and fly off to begin a new life where we cannot reach him. He may not have realized yet,' the man added grimly, 'that no such place exists on earth. On the moon, perhaps. However, we would prefer that you deliver the money directly to us, letting Mr Brora remain heavily in our debt.' He smiled again. Alice had seen a crocodile in the zoo smile with distinctly less menace. 'In the circumstances we could afford to be more generous than Mr Brora. We might say ... twelve per cent? That should allow you a margin for making your own getaway.'

Alice was thinking rapidly. These visitors, presumably, represented the drug barons who had suffered the original loss. By now, Jock Brora would know that they had no intention of passing over Mona Lisa's money to him, but he had not admitted the fact to his creditors. Or else, she realized suddenly, the visitors had taken several days to track them down and their information was seriously out of date.

During the silence, the man's patience had worn thin. 'We will deal with the matter here and now,' he said, 'and then all unpleasantness will be behind us. You have your computer and a telephone. Make the transfers now.'

'We can't,' Sarah said.

The atmosphere in the small room shifted instantly from vague menace to acute danger. 'I think you can. You have been proceeding by e-mail. You ladies are younger than the man, you would be more familiar with this technology.'

'The older man that you know about,' Alice said. The words came out distorted by her fear. She paused and swallowed. 'He did the banking by telephone. Even if we knew the techniques, we don't know the passwords and PIN numbers. We don't even know which banks the money is in.'

'I do not believe you. For your sakes I hope that you are lying. There are ways of getting at the truth. You might consider them very unpleasant, although I, for one, usually enjoy them.' He nodded to his companion.

The chill in the man's voice convinced Alice that he was sincere and she felt her fear increase until it was like an icy spray on her back. What she had said was perfectly true, but even if they had been able and willing to transfer Mona Lisa's money it seemed unlikely that their lives would be spared. It all depended now on her father. Although she knew better than to take a direct look, Alice had been aware in her peripheral vision of paleness in the darkness outside, a small lightening of the gloom, which had to be her father's face. He was standing well back from the window, but the window was open slightly at the top and she was sure that he could hear every word. He had said that he was not a man of violence but she knew that he could be violent when the time was right. Now, she thought, would be a very good time.

While the other man stood with his back to the door, Mr Dunwoodie's options were limited; but as the big man stepped forward, feeling in his pocket with his free hand, the door burst inward. Alice's father had armed himself with a stout length of timber, part of a broken oar that he had retained for use as a lever. The big man, caught with his gun hand pointing in the opposite direction and his left hand in his pocket, could neither turn quickly enough to meet the new threat nor parry the broken oar. A blow to the back of his head put him down though not out. His hand came out of his pocket with a ball of stout cord. The revolver clattered away across the floor. The oar had suffered a second fracture in the impact. It was now much reduced in value as a weapon and Mr Dunwoodie tossed it into a corner of the room.

Alice found a new respect for her father. The leader of the two intruders moved in quickly and swung a punch which was blocked. He tried a knee to the groin that was parried by a quickly raised thigh. Then he was spun and held, face to the wall, in a simple hammerlock held on one-handed. Mr Dunwoodie fumbled a key out of his pocket and tossed it to Alice. 'Out to the cars,' he snapped.

Sarah was already out of her chair. Possessing very few pockets but a multiplicity of handbags, she was in the habit of leaving the key to her MG on the nearest convenient surface to the door. She had it in her hand and was out of that door in a flash with Alice on her heels. Alice could already see the advantage of getting both cars on the move. 'They can't follow both of us,' she said. 'Head for my parents' home. We'll join you there.'

'Right.'

After the lights in the cottage, the night was as black as a deserted coal mine. Alice found the Rover by the gleams on the bodywork. She fumbled for the keyhole and started the engine just as Sarah's MG spurted off into the dark. By the car's lights, she saw that a Range Rover had been parked between the other cars. With its large engine, high ground clearance and four-wheel drive, it would have the legs of either the MG or Mr Dunwoodie's Rover, especially over the rough and sandy ground. Would they shoot? Would they force the car off the road and into the trees? Or were they incapacitated?

As she backed the Rover in a semi-circle, her father came racing out of the cottage and threw himself into the front passenger seat. The two dogs leaped on top of him and over into the back of the car. 'Get going,' Mr Dunwoodie said.

Alice got going. 'You didn't kill them, then?'

'No.'

'Why not?'

'I don't kill people.'

Well, it was a point of view. Alice had a mental picture of the two visitors searching the cottage, plumbing their secrets and possibly torching the building. It hit her like a hammer-blow to realize that fear had outrun instinct and that Hugh was still asleep in the bedroom. If the men stopped to regroup, Hugh would make the perfect hostage. It was almost a relief to see the Range Rover's lights in her mirror. Almost but not quite. A ruthless man at the wheel of a Range Rover could run either of the other cars off the road. Sarah's lights were already vanishing along the track.

Alice's one advantage, she realized immediately, was that she knew the geography. During the early part of her father's incarceration, while she and Justin had still been at the stage of courtship, she had used the Rover to visit the cottage in order to collect some personal gear and to shut the place up. Justin had arrived to help her in his own car and the two finished in high spirits with several races on the beach.

She spun the wheel and headed for the gap between two dunes.

'What the hell are you *doing*?'

'Trust me,' she said anxiously. If the Range Rover turned to follow the MG, she would have to do the same. The big car would easily have overhauled Sarah before she could have reached the main road. It would all have ended in a stupendous mess. But to her huge relief the lights of the Range Rover swept round, bounced as the car picked up speed on the undulating ground but settled blazing into her mirror.

The sandy ground was reinforced by coarse grass and the Rover kept its momentum, pitching through the undulations like a boat at sea. Alice had learned several lessons about handling a car on sand. She kept up her speed without ever using too much throttle or turning the wheel by more than a touch. They emerged on to the soft sand above the tide line and she took the shortest route towards where a margin of darker sand a quarter of a mile wide showed where the sea had been a few hours earlier. The tide, she thought, would have started to flood again.

The Range Rover, with its four-wheel drive, was gaining ground. Alice lost time to wheelspin and she had to ignore the onset of panic. But they came on to the darker sand. She put her foot down and slewed the car round to run along the beach. Almost immediately, the Range Rover was again blazing lights into her mirror, but it was no longer catching up. She took one hand off the wheel to knock the main mirror aside, leaned forward to exclude the reflections from the door mirrors and strained her eyes. The Rover's lights were good, but not quite good enough. She lifted her foot slightly and angled down towards the sea. The driver of the other vehicle took the hint and came up on that side to cut off what he assumed to be her desired line to pass some obstacle.

The landmark that she watched for, a low hump of rock at the top of the beach, showed suddenly. She held on for another tense second and then braked, turned the wheel and accelerated hard. Her father was saying something, or perhaps he was only making concerned noises, she was too busy to listen. The car fought its way round, spraying sand, teetered on a brink but recovered and kept going, heading inland.

Near the rocks, a burn – a stream – emerged. It had been almost invisible from their low angle, but when in spate it was a torrent and it had cut itself a deep gully through the sand. Alice's violent turn had brought her round just short of its bank, but the other driver was caught off-guard. His lights continued, dropped and became a vanishing glow. A flash of mistiness must have been spray caught in the Range Rover's lights as it plunged into ten feet of salt water.

Alice was peering ahead, looking for the mouth of a track that ran towards the main road.

'Better get back to the cottage and gather our things,' said Mr Dunwoodie.

'But not along the beach,' Alice said. 'We could just as easily stick. I'll take the long way round. We can still be there and gone before they could run along the beach. They'll never get their car out from where it is.'

'True, I hope,' said her father. Alice thought that he was having difficulty controlling his voice.

Weeks later, checking back on the wording

of one of Justin's advertisements, she came across a sidebar in a Scottish paper, about two men being found drowned in a car off some unspecified but remote beach. By then, it was much too late to worry about it.

They retrieved their luggage and papers from the cottage and left it secure and dark. Hugh went into the car, still deeply asleep and quite unaware of all the excitement. They worked in haste in case the two men managed to make a return before they finished, but there was no sign of interruption. The roads, when they reached them, were dark and empty.

Sarah was waiting in her car outside the Dunwoodie residence. After a quick conference, it was decided that the night was almost gone. An early arrival at Angus Castle would be acceptable and safe. Sarah and Mr Dunwoodie decided to sleep the rest of the night away in his house.

Alice, Hugh and Humph were deposited at their home. Alice let herself in and moved the luggage into the hall. She thought that she had moved in total silence, but Hugh had woken suddenly and decided that it was time for an extra feed. The whimper aroused Justin and he appeared suddenly in the kitchen door, tousled and half-asleep. He awoke enough to clasp Alice around the waist, swing her off her feet and kiss her thoroughly. 'God, it's good to have you back,' he said.

Alice had no objection to this display of enthusiasm, but it would have been unwise to let him think that her return was permanent. 'Make the most of me,' she said. 'I'll have to go off again today. Will you feed Hugh while I get a midnight snack ready?'

Justin sat down, accepted the wriggling bundle and began to spoon milky mush into his firstborn. 'Isn't the boat finished?' he asked.

'It's in beautiful shape,' Alice said with perfect truth. She then let truth fly out of the window. 'I had a chat with Mona Lisa when she came into the shop,' she said. 'We were very much on the same wavelength. She phoned me last night. She wants me to go and stay at Castle Angus for a while. She wants somebody she knows and trusts to be there, to supervise the preparations for her wedding. I'll leave Humph with you for company and to keep you out of mischief. You know that he tells me everything. Don't panic,' Alice added quickly as Justin's hair began to register disquiet. 'I'll stock you up with lots of easy frozen meals and I can pop back for a night now and again to do your laundry and attend to your little comforts. She's paying me a handsome fee, so you can afford to take on a temp to do your typing and filing. I'll catch up again with the accounts and VAT when the fuss has died down.'

Justin looked sharply at his wife. But she had promised faithfully that her days of adventuring beyond the law were behind her and they had agreed to trust each other. His hair settled down. 'I can go along with that,' he said.

'Have you sent off her lockplates?'

'Days ago. They'll have been colour-hardened by now.'

That was a relief. If Mona Lisa had visited the shop again for another look at her engraving, an incautious word might have set Justin on the track.

'Did she pay you for the engraving?'

'I get paid through the gun-makers, but she's paid them and they've coughed up like gentlemen.'

'Fine. So let's put Buggins to bed. Then we can enjoy our snack and make use of what's left of the night.'

Justin laid Hugh down gently in his carrycot and pulled Alice against him. 'Do you mean what I hope you mean?' he asked.

'More than that,' Alice said. 'Much more than that. Beyond your wildest dreams. It's my firm intention that you won't be able to get it up again until I come back.'

'You can count on my enthusiastic help,' Justin said.

Eight

Alice found her first sight of Castle Angus overpowering.

During the seventeenth and eighteenth centuries, the family had had a finger in every profitable pie but, unlike many another, without ever getting a finger burnt. Substantial estates in the West Indies had been supplied with labour by investment in the slave trade. The same ships had brought back sugar and rum from the plantations and had run certain highly desirable cargoes to the continental harbours from which smaller vessels smuggled it past the Revenue cutters. The profits were ploughed back, mostly into land.

The eighth earl had found himself with more land and money than he knew what to do with. Having a fancy to entertain royalty on the grand scale, he had added, to an old but already sizeable castle set in the comparatively lush countryside of east central

Scotland, what was in effect a minor palace modelled loosely on Versailles – indeed, Alice thought, the many turrets looked French rather than Scottish. The building had been designed with taste and common sense so that, though there could be no doubt where the ancient castle and the modern building joined, the two lived harmoniously together. Wars, death duties, gambling and an ambitious programme of modernization had eroded the family fortunes and much of the land had been sold off in the interest of survival. The castle and the reduced estates remained the property of the current earl and, to meet the enormous running cost, the diminished income was supplemented by guided tours for the public on Tuesdays and Thursdays and by letting the castle for conferences, exhibitions, promotions, weddings and other events, all right at the very top end of the market. The amenities were supplemented by tennis courts, stables and a nine-hole golf course which, because green fees on the only full-length course within convenient motoring distance were beyond the average pocket, was the province and responsibility of a local club, the amenity being shared by the castle.

The huge portico was approached at first between wide lawns backed by massed ranks of rhododendrons. The imposing frontage was flanked by the high walls enclosing the protected part of the castle gardens and grounds. Apparently the non-paying visitor was to be denied sight of the proper gardens. Discreet signs directed the motorist to the visitors' car parks but Mr Dunwoodie stopped uncompromisingly before the great doors. Sarah's MG drew up behind them.

Hugh was sound asleep, so Alice left him in the Rover with the radio baby alarm attached to the carrycot. By dispensation obtained over the telephone, Suzy was to be allowed to accompany the party (but subject to banishment to the castle kennels on occasions) and Alice knew that Hugh would be safe with such a guardian. The receiver in her pocket she switched on. As they climbed the steps, one of a pair of doors, which would almost have admitted a double-decker bus, opened. The man who, although he wore a grey cardigan in place of the formal coat, could only have been a butler or major-domo, waited, eyebrows politely raised.

Sarah had met this formidable being already. 'Good morning, Laurie,' she said.

'This is Mr Dunwoodie and Mrs Dennison. We're expected.'

Laurie bowed slightly. 'Miss McLeod. Madam. Sir. Step this way please. Gordon will attend to your luggage. Your car keys, please.'

As a young man in a short, black jacket and striped trousers appeared from behind Laurie and hurried down the steps, the party, properly intimidated, followed Laurie through a massive entrance hall. Alice had an impression of doors of plate glass and polished mahogany leading off into even vaster ranges of awe-inspiring rooms, but they were led through a smaller and less conspicuous door and along a passage. This soon altered in character and, from the smallness of the windows and the thickness of the walls, Alice guessed that they were entering part of the original castle proper. The floor changed from parquet to linoleum, but of very high quality.

Several doors opened out of a small lobby. Mr Laurie opened a glass-panelled door into an office the size of two squash courts and announced the party with a resonance more suited to the arrival of royalty at a grand ball.

Of the four businesslike desks in the room,

two were empty and one was occupied by an elderly typist who glanced up from her work, smiled sweetly and then returned to her typing. Rising to her feet behind the fourth desk was a woman of about thirty, neatly dressed in a grey business suit. Behind careful make-up she had a masculine face lacking any pretensions to beauty, but a glossy mane of jet-black hair redeemed her appearance. She came forward to shake hands. Sarah introduced her companions. 'This is Miss Evans,' she explained. 'The castle's business manager.'

'The castle's very recently appointed business manager,' said Miss Evans, smiling distantly. 'To be honest, I was not in favour of accepting another major function at such short notice before I had had time to pick up the reins but I was overruled.'

'That's largely why we're here,' Mr Dunwoodie said.

Miss Evans nodded as if the comment had been too obvious to be worth making. 'It was clear that you'd already got the work well in hand,' she said.

'And I'm sure that Tom can keep us all straight,' said Sarah. 'Is he not here?'

'His Lordship is somewhere about,' Miss Evans said. 'Ah, here he is.'

His Lordship, who must have arrived quietly in the lobby through one of the other doors, appeared as suddenly as a demon from a trap. He was a distinguished-looking man. Sarah had described him as being in his late forties or early fifties but Alice decided that the earl was still well short of his half-century. A full head of silvered hair was neatly trimmed and he had a moustache to match. His face was benign but his eyes were shrewd. In spite of the passage of time and the inheritance of what would seem to most observers to be great wealth, he had not lost his figure; Alice put this down to his air of restrained energy. Like his butler, he wore an old cardigan over his formal clothes; Alice guessed that suitable coats and jackets were hanging in some secret cupboard off the hall and that the arrival of royalty or even the Second Coming would not catch the household unready.

He advanced on Sarah with his hand outstretched. 'Ah,' he said warmly. 'Miss McLeod. It's good to see you again.' His voice was well modulated but his accent was absolutely neutral.

Sarah was dumbstruck. She was evidently overcome to realize that she had been on first name and mildly flirtatious terms with an earl. Alice, for her part, was suddenly uncertain how to address an earl as opposed to a judge or a bishop. It was left to Mr Dunwoodie, who was rarely at a loss, to introduce himself and his daughter, using just the right blend of friendly deference.

The earl listened for a moment – just long enough, Alice decided, to evaluate the arrivals by their immediate reactions – and then smiled affably. 'Since you come bearing lots of much needed money,' he said, 'I think you could all call me Tom. One thing we're not short of here is rooms, so we've put the office next door at your disposal. Your luggage will be in your bedrooms. You'll want to settle in. Then—' he glanced at his watch – 'please join me for lunch. Just ring and somebody will come and fetch you.'

The butler, Laurie, reappeared and led them up a winding stair to the three bedrooms allocated to them. Mr Dunwoodie had a word with Laurie and money changed hands discreetly. Considering the scale of the building, the rooms were smaller than Alice had expected, although each had facilities *en suite* in what had once been an enormous wardrobe or robing room. Laurie confirmed that they were still in the original part of the castle where the bedrooms were reserved for family and their guests and were rarely let. To her surprise, Hugh, still deeply asleep, had been brought up along with the luggage and Suzy was lying with her eyes on the carrycot. From the window she had an oblique view of part of the castle gardens, which seemed to range over an enormous area and yet to be enclosed by the continuous high stone wall. Within the wall but close to the castle was tarmac holding a number of cars. Alice could make out Sarah's yellow MG.

When she had washed and tidied herself, Alice transferred the receiver of the baby alarm from her coat pocket to the belt of her dress and she was ready. Gordon, presumably a footman (although in this household he might equally have been heir to the earldom), brought them down to a room which would have seated twelve. In most homes, this would have been a generous dining room, but Alice guessed that there would be another and larger private dining room reserved for the family. Miss Evans joined them. There were only five at the table.

The meal was simple, served by a maid in an apron over an everyday dress, but the earl was a good though unpretentious host. He devoted some of the meal to an exposition of the geography and facilities of the castle. Over coffee and cheese he said, 'Of course, it's impossible to keep a place this size continuously busy, so we can't keep it permanently staffed on the scale that's needed for major events. We use a contract firm to clean when required and we're fortunate in having an army of locals available on call to act as maids and waiters and so on.'

'But surely,' Sarah said, 'that wouldn't be economic for ongoing work? Don't you have permanent staff for maintenance? And the gardens?'

'Quite right,' said the earl. He gave her a look in which appraisal and appreciation were nicely balanced. 'We have gardeners, keepers, maintenance tradesmen and some jacks-of-all-trades. We don't encourage restrictive practices here – everybody turns his hand to what's needed next. Most seem to find it a refreshing change to do somebody else's job for a while.'

Alice had one or two questions to ask about this seemingly idyllic state of affairs, but a sudden noise from her waist level told the world that Hugh had woken up and found himself hungry and alone. 'You'll have to excuse me,' she said. 'Motherhood

150

calls. I'll join you in our new office as soon as I can.'

The human animal, even in infancy, requires more than mere food and sleep. Washed, changed, fed and relieved of any residual gasses, Hugh was still unwilling to be returned to sleep. But there was much to do and far less than the usually required time to do it in, so that time would soon press. Alice sighed and lugged him in his carrycot down the winding stair and into the room set aside for their use.

The single large table was already half covered with papers, mobile phones, two landline phones with a telephone amplifier and the laptop computer with its printer. Her father, Sarah, Miss Evans and the earl were already gathered round the table.

Mr Dunwoodie looked without favour at his only grandchild. 'We would have been here hours earlier,' he said, 'but for the demands of that child and the need to gather up and transport a mountain of chattels for its maintenance and support. Is there no end to its claim on your time?'

Alice knew that when her father waxed grandiloquent he was on the verge of becoming irritable. She refused to be ruffled and she was now confident that she could match her father, rolling period for rolling period, any time that he cared to become pompous. 'No,' she said. 'And may I remind you that it was you who invited me to get involved in an operation which seems to rival the Normandy landings in logistical complexity. Although why we make such a ritual out of what somebody – Oscar Wilde? – called something like *a ghastly public declaration of a strictly private intention* escapes me. My own nuptials, you may recall, were comparatively modest. However, if you would prefer that I withdraw, taking your grandson with me, I shall be pleased to do so.' She dumped Hugh on her father's lap.

Miss Evans and the earl were hiding smiles. Sarah, openly grinning, said, 'Don't desert us now. You did more than your share of the masterminding so far.'

Mr Dunwoodie accepted his grandson with a good grace and smiled to show that there were few if any hard feelings. 'You take me too literally,' he said.

'Now that that's out of the way,' Alice said, 'we should get moving. If there's to be an announcement tomorrow we can start to phone at last without fear of breaching confidentiality. It's time we spoke with the bride.'

'You do that,' Sarah said. 'You've met her.'

'Right. Then you could call up the e-mails and see what replies have come in with quotations. We'll arrange it all into a detailed plan of action as we go along.'

'Which,' the earl said in the direction of Miss Evans, 'would seem to make us *de trop* for the moment. Call on us for local knowledge.'

Miss Evans nodded. 'I'll be next door whenever I'm needed.'

Hugh had decided that business conferences were not his scene at all. He began to grizzle.

The earl was fond of children and it was a source of discontent for him that his only son was raising a brood in South Africa. His wife, he had explained over lunch, had died some years earlier. 'I have nothing much to do for the next hour or so,' he said, 'and there's a pram kept here in readiness for visits from my younger relatives. May I suggest...?'

And so it happened that, after suitable but insincere protests, Hugh was wheeled around the gardens by a member of the House of Lords while his mother and grandfather got down to work.

Alice was relieved that the earl's tactful withdrawal let her make her first call without curious ears in the room. She only had a mobile number for Mona Lisa but the singer's mellow voice answered the phone's ringing almost instantly. 'Good afternoon,' Alice said. 'I'm speaking from Castle Angus. We had your e-mail and we assume that secrecy is no longer of the essence.'

'That's so. The press releases went out, embargoed until tomorrow morning.'

'Fine. So can we check over some of the necessary steps?'

'Just at the moment I'm up to my bum in the River Dee. I'll call you back in half an hour.'

'Fine,' said Alice. 'How's the fishing?'

'A dead loss. The river's low and there's hardly a fish in it.'

'Cheer up, there's rain forecast.'

'It can't come too soon. Hey, your voice sounds kind of familiar. Have we met?' There was a sloshing sound, which Alice interpreted as being caused by the singer wading to the bank.

'Once,' Alice said. 'I'm Mrs Dennison. My husband engraved your guns. Clever of you to remember.'

'Voices are my stock-in-trade. Your husband's a genius. I'll get back to you.'

Alice breathed more easily. With Castle Angus believing that they were employed by Mona Lisa and with the singer being under the impression that they worked for the castle, she had been wondering how to resolve the dangerous impasse; but it seemed that they were being taken on trust. The truth, if it ever emerged, might be embarrassing but it would no longer be incriminating.

The list of quotations was nearing completion when Mona Lisa phoned. The tune on the mobile phone coincided with the return of the earl carrying Hugh. The timbre of the singer's voice had changed and Alice decided that she had probably returned to her hotel room.

'OK now,' said Mona Lisa. 'Fire away.'

The telephone amplifier had a suction cup attachment for mobile phones. Alice connected it and switched it on. 'Will you make a note of a new e-mail address and phone numbers?'

'Let's have them ... OK. What's next?'

Alice looked at the top item on the checklist. 'You've had the banns read or posted?'

There was a pause long enough for Alice

to meet three pairs of eyes – not counting Hugh's. 'Holy hell!' The singer's voice came through loud and clear. 'I'd forgotten all about it. I've spent a lot of time in the States and I've got accustomed to my friends marrying and divorcing at the drop of a hat. How long notice is needed?'

'Fifteen days,' Alice said.

'Oops! You seemed so much on the ball that I've been letting things slide, just breezing along and waiting for the Happy Day. I forgot there were things I had to do. I've ordered a dress and that's about it. Well, we've got our fifteen days and not a lot left over. What do we do?'

Alice hesitated. The earl handed over Hugh to Sarah and held out his hand for the phone. 'Here's the Earl of Angus,' Alice said. 'It's his castle and he knows about weddings and things.'

The earl took the phone. 'Hullo. Are you a UK resident?'

'Yes, Lord Brechin.' (Alice raised her eyebrows respectfully. Evidently Mona Lisa had not let things slide altogether. Shehad done her homework with surprising thoroughness.)

'Call me Tom – everyone else does. Well, that's a help. And your fiancé?'

'He's a US citizen.'

'Has he been married before?'

'No.'

'If he had, your wedding would definitely have had to be postponed.' The earl paused to gather his thoughts but it was obvious that he was no novice at arranging weddings. 'Go to the nearest registrar of births, marriages and deaths. The address should be in the telephone directory. You want a Marriage Notice Form for each of you. As well as filling out that form, your fiancé will also need a Certificate Of No Impediment issued by the civil authority wherever he lives. And both your birth certificates will be required. How quickly could you do all that by mail?'

Mona Lisa could be heard to sigh. 'The way the mails are these days, with every item being X-rayed for explosives or examined for terrorist materials, it could take a month. And he can't knock off and fly over here in the later stages of making a film. I'll phone him to start the ball rolling while I fly over there. If I can catch tomorrow's Concorde, I'll be back Saturday night. And then I'd better be available to answer questions. Can you provide me with a room?'

The earl laughed. 'I can give you your

choice from several hundred. We can find you some fishing to replace what you'll miss, but I think you'll find that you're too busy. Fly in to Edinburgh or Aberdeen; tell us your time of arrival and you'll be collected from Dyce Airport or Turnhouse.'

'Thank you, Tom. Any other urgent questions?'

The earl looked at Alice who had to pull her wits together. She had been momentarily dumbstruck by the talk of casually flying to and fro across the Atlantic. She spoke into the amplifier. 'Civil service or religious?' she asked.

'We're neither of us great churchgoers. Civil.'

'Invitations?'

'A secretarial agency. They should have been posted yesterday.'

Alice ran her pencil rapidly down the margin of her list. 'There's nothing else that can't wait until Saturday,' she said.

'I'll speak to the local registrars,' said the earl, 'warn them that the papers are on the way and make sure that somebody's available on the day. Keep your cellphone alive so that we can contact you if anything else arises. *Bon voyage.*'

* * *

The rhythm of the days was soon established. The earl, it transpired, piloted his own light plane and was often away in Edinburgh or London; but when he was present the group was usually invited to dine with him and any of his young cousins who might be making one of their rare visits. When available, he was a tower of strength. He seemed to know from past experience which suppliers were unreliable and which could be relied on to deliver on time and at the quoted price. He knew whom to approach for the hire of extra tables and chairs. He called in a lady who could be trusted to find accommodation for overflow guests, visiting servitors and the personal maids and other dogsbodies of the wedding guests. By longstanding arrangement, in preference to hiring a firm of caterers, he recommended a retired chef who could muster the necessary catering staff for the castle kitchens. Laurie, the butler, was expert at summoning and organizing the waiters. And so it went on. As the little team coalesced, Mr Dunwoodie took over the logistics and supplies, Alice attended to the programming of events and Sarah kept control of expenditure and accounts.

On the morning of their first full day at the

castle, the media were filled with announcements of the forthcoming event – the weightier journals relegating it to a filler or sidebar and the more frivolous devoting pages of speculation to what would undoubtedly be the show-business wedding of the year if not of the decade. They were limited, for the moment, to the first of a series of carefully discreet press releases. Security measures were triggered immediately and journalists were turned away empty-handed. Persistent celeb-watchers hung around the portico and the entry gates to the enclosed grounds. One, indeed, set up house in a motor caravan almost on the earl's doorstep but an enormous recovery vehicle materialized and he found himself deposited, still in his Dormobile, on the verge beside the main road.

They had continued secretly to monitor Gus Castle's e-mail address and next morning it carried a message. *Last chance*, it read. *The whole sum now or the beans get spilled.*

'Jock Brora will be panicking,' Mr Dunwoodie said. 'Well, let him panic. As we know, Jock owes a mountain of money that he doesn't possess to some very hard men indeed. Well, tough! If you play with the big boys you must expect bruises when you lose.

I don't think that we should dignify the cheap attempt at blackmail with a reply.'

Alice looked at him sharply but he was quite serious. This was the pot condemning the kettle with a vegeance. 'He won't take it out on Justin, will he?' she asked anxiously.

'Not a chance. Jock knows as well as I do that revenge pays no dividends, that it can only start a feud and that it gives no satisfaction if it's applied to a proxy. What's more, it's years since he did his own violence and if he has money troubles his soldiers will soon be going AWOL.'

Despite the reassurance, Alice still felt a trace of anxiety that no amount of evening telephoning could assuage. On the afternoon of the following day, she borrowed Sarah's car, loaded Hugh and his necessities and went home for the night to a rapturous welcome from Humph and a scarcely more restrained greeting from Justin. Sliding easily into her hyperactive mode, she blasted through the outstanding administration at Justin's business, stormed round the house reimposing order and hygiene, conjured a meal on to the table, consigned Hugh to his bed and then coaxed a tired but grateful husband into fresh, amorous life. Alice remained determined that, in her absence,

Justin would not be exposed to temptation – or, if exposed, would not be capable of yielding to it. Her deliciously refined ministrations proved anew that absence does indeed inject additional fondness into the heart – and other organs.

Over breakfast, they had time to talk. Justin asked how the wedding preparations were coming along.

'I think we're doing well,' Alice said. 'It should take months to set up an event like this but we're getting by. The invitations have gone out, so if there's any legal hiccup they'll have a terrible job cancelling or postponing. She thinks you're a genius, by the way.'

Justin's smile, as usual, gave his normally unemotional face an expression that Alice, in her lonelier moments, tried unsuccessfully to conjure up. 'I agree with her,' he said. 'How long will you be away this time?'

'I don't know. Until the wedding, I expect. I'll keep popping back. Do you mind being left to fend for yourself?'

'Provided that we always celebrate your return as we did last night,' Justin said, 'go as often as you like.' He yawned hugely.

Justin, who was busy on the Celtic engraving

of a set of vessels for a new church in Glasgow, hurried away and Alice, after giving Humph a hasty walk in the park, set off back to Castle Angus. The forecast rain had passed through in the night and there was freshness in the air. She put the top down and enjoyed the journey while making sure that Hugh was not being chilled. She was in the castle drive with the portico in view when a police Range Rover met and passed her.

Laurie was still struggling with the heavy door but Alice drove round the flank of the castle to one of the few gates in the wall surrounding the castle grounds. Several journalists of more than normal persistence were being kept at bay by the security guards but Alice was admitted. A broad terrace lay behind the castle but one end of this was taken up by the hard standing that Alice had seen from her window. She parked the MG between her father's Rover and the several cars belonging to the castle, reminding herself to be very surprised at any news of police interest. In the office, she found the earl with her father, Miss Evans and Sarah. She put the carrycot down on the side table where Hugh slept away much of his time. 'I saw a police car,' she said. 'Was that about security?'

Lord Brechin, Earl of Angus, had got up to chirrup over Hugh, with whom he seemed to be developing a special relationship, but he looked up and answered. 'We got around to security and traffic management in the end,' he said. 'But that wasn't what they came for. Apparently some idiot gave them a hint that Mona Lisa was being defrauded. I had to bring them in here, show them some of the correspondence and assure them that we had received a very substantial deposit.' He sighed and then chuckled. 'Some people get weird bees in their bonnets, don't they, young fellow?'

Hugh made a gurgling sound that was generally taken to be of assent.

Miss Evans, as was proper in one who had come very new to a complex job, listened more than she uttered, but for once she spoke up. 'All the same,' she said in her sing-song Welsh voice, 'I wonder what put that idea into somebody's mind.'

Mona Lisa returned as promised on the Saturday evening. The earl flew down to Edinburgh to collect her from Turnhouse Airport. He told Sarah later that he could hardly get the light aircraft off the tarmac for the weight of the singer's luggage, which took two gardeners half an hour to carry up from the castle airstrip. A photographer seemed to have set up house in a tree that overlooked the airstrip but a cunningly placed and suddenly fired-up bonfire spoiled his chance.

Among her luggage was the singer's jewellery and her most immediate concern was for strongroom accommodation for it. As she explained over dinner that first evening, 'For more years than I care to remember, people have been throwing money at me. I never asked for the half of it, but I have an agent on percentage whose pedigree is by shark out of vulture. He eats and breathes money and whenever I think that "That's it, we've peaked and from here on it's all downhill", he signs another and bigger deal and the bonanza redoubles.' She was speaking factually without boasting, leaning back in her chair with a glass of wine in her hand. She was still only a shadow of the spectacular performer to be seen on stage. Her dress was formal but plain, embellished by a single strand of pearls, and her hair was short and simply dressed, in contrast to the flamboyant wig that she wore on stage. But in the soft light she was almost beautiful.

'Well, I'll never spend the tenth of it and I don't go in for a lot of minders and managers, just a secretary who does my managing for me. I've bought some property, but one investment I can make that I can keep under my own hand and be damn sure that I'm not being ripped off by a string of managers is jewellery. I never add up what I've spent, but the insured total frightens me stupid. I know a dealer who was a good friend of my father, and most of what I've bought has turned out to be sound investment. But that isn't what it's for. I buy jewellery because it's a thrill to acquire things of such beauty. I never wear much of it – what you see on stage or the telly is paste – but if I'm ever going to show some of it off, surely my wedding is the right time and place?'

There was general agreement and a stirring of interest. The earl had already provided safe storage in the cellars beneath the old castle, where the walls were three feet thick and the doors were four inches of oak. Those doors, he explained, might be several hundred years old but they were in view of the security sensors and the locks were new. He promised to evict some of his own treasures from their robust glass cases so that the jewellery could be put on show.

'Do you intend to allow the press in for the wedding?' the earl asked.

The singer shook her head. 'My agent's done an exclusive deal with one of the gossip magazines.'

'Of course,' Sarah said, 'that should offset some of what you're spending.'

Mona Lisa looked at her sharply. 'This is my wedding,' she said. 'It's a one-off event and I don't want it spoiled by a lot of commercialization. The magazine's paying a bundle of lucre, but it goes to the Show Business Benevolent Fund.'

Sarah mumbled an apology.

'It was a rational assumption.' Mona Lisa sighed with pleasure. 'I always fancied being married here since I came once before to sing.'

'That was an occasion I remember well,' the earl said. He looked round the table. 'Pavilion Opera were putting on *Il Trovatore* in the ballroom. Their Gilda fell ill at the last moment and the understudy caught the same flu bug. Mona Lisa stood in at very short notice and did the whole performance, exquisitely, with the book in her hand, sight-reading all the way. It was a momentous performance and I've been a devoted fan ever since.'

'I nearly blew it more than once,' the singer said. 'There had been no time for rehearsals. I had an earpiece telling me which moves to make, and the rest of the cast had to take their time from me. I never worked so hard in my life, but Angus Castle struck me as the perfect venue for another and very special sort of occasion. I never thought that it would happen for me, but you're all making my dream come true.'

Nine

With the arrival of Mona Lisa, life within the castle acquired a fresh sparkle. Unlike many entertainers who can only shine in the light of audience adulation, she was naturally ebullient and her good cheer soon infected her companions. Even the usually taciturn Miss Evans unwound enough to recount a not very funny event from her past.

But there was little uncommitted time for enjoying the jolly atmosphere. With the bride now available to give decisions on a thousand questions and with the Great Day looming ever closer, teamwork was necessary and plenty of it. Their roles were clear. Mr Dunwoodie, in liaison with the earl, took responsibility for the transport of guests and personnel and for accommodation, dispersal and parking. The same two had the final choice, subject only to the bride herself, in the selection of the suppliers of services and goods. Sarah then placed the orders, received and checked the wines and other supplies and would later check them out to the caterers. She settled the accounts and prepared a final tally for Mona Lisa. Alice prepared, amended, timed and amplified the masterplan for the three crucial days, determining who and what would be where and when, and exactly how it or they should arrive there. Miss Evans, under the earl's supervision, organized the implementation of the masterplan by the castle's staff and contractors, but from time to time it seemed that only the earl's frequent checks on her efforts averted some logistical disaster. The visitors soon noticed that friction was developing between the new castle manager and her employer. It was assumed that her reign would be brief.

Mona Lisa was unavailable to most of the team on the morning after her arrival, which she spent with the earl and the registrar, ironing out any remaining wrinkles from the legalities. After that, Alice claimed her attention. Alice's first session with Mona Lisa was hard work. Although aware of the urgency, the singer was inclined to digress. Her showbusiness anecdotes were so amusing, and often so scandalous, that Alice never had the heart to interrupt her. Other digressions

slowed their progress. When Alice mentioned in passing that at one time there had been
a fashion for greeting each guest on arrival
with five sugared almonds in a twist of
muslin, the bride was immediately determined to follow that tradition. 'Leave it with
me,' she said. 'I have a friend in the sweet
business. What's next?'

'Let's get back to basics,' Alice said. Fun-
time had to be over or the wedding would be
a rout. The plans of the castle were spread
out before them. 'The castle chapel isn't
large enough for so many guests. You can get
married in the ballroom and the company
can go straight to lunch while the chairs are
cleared. Or you can marry in the chapel with
family and the closer of your friends present
and the remainder of the guests can follow
the ceremony on a big screen in the ballroom, standing around with Champagne in
their hands.'

A short break was necessary, during which
Mona Lisa visited and approved the chapel,
subject to the importation of flowers to
brighten the bare chamber. When they had
settled again she said, 'Knowing Craig's
friends, they'd rather stay where the drink is.
We'll use the chapel option.'

Alice made a note to seek quotes for an

enormous video screen for the ballroom. 'Then after the signing of the register *here*, assuming that the day's dry, we thought the guests could be fed more Champagne on the terrace *here* and we'd sneak you round by this passage to appear *here* and shake hands with the guests as they go in to lunch by way of the marquee.'

The singer thought it over, tracing the route with her finger, and then nodded. 'I can't quarrel with that. What if it rains?'

'Then they have their Champagne in the ballroom, we sneak you round *this* way and you do your kissing and handshaking bit in the doorway between there and the dining room. Mr Laurie will have his hands full. Shall we have the castle engage the services of whichever toastmaster they usually use?'

'Go right ahead.'

Alice made another note. 'We'll need to know the number of acceptances as soon as you do.'

'They're going direct to Juliana, my secretary, housekeeper and everything else. She'll e-mail me the list as far as it's gone in a couple of days and come to join me for the wedding. Will you make sure there's a room for her?'

'Include her on the guest list,' Alice said.

'Which reminds me. What about the rest of your entourage? Surely it's unknown for a celebrity to appear in public without a tail like a comet?'

'It seems to me,' said the singer, 'that you have to feel very insecure to need that kind of ego-bolstering.'

'I suppose that's true,' Alice said. 'If you have the talent instead.'

Mona Lisa looked amused. 'You mean the ego comes with the job?' she asked.

'I don't mean any such thing,' Alice said. She realized that Mona Lisa was laughing at her. 'And you know it.' She produced and unfolded a large sheet of paper. 'This is a print of the table layout they've used before. If you agree it, you'll have to do the seating plan.'

The singer was beginning to look frayed. 'Can't you do that for me?'

'I suppose so – if you give us your list in order of importance and also warn us of any guests who should be kept apart – Jews and Arabs for instance, and couples who should sit or sleep together.'

This was the signal for another of Mona Lisa's digressions. 'While I was in New York the other day,' she said, 'I saw a sign in a shop window. It said, *We would rather serve one Arab terrorist than a hundred Jews.'*

'Wow! New York's full of Jews,' Alice said. 'Didn't the place get ostracized or bombed or something?'

'No. The place was Goldstein's Funeral Parlour.' They laughed together. 'The top table could be cut down. Eight places would be enough. My big sister's coming. She's a lawyer in New Zealand.'

'Married?'

'Not that I've heard so far.'

Alice had picked up one little gem from the wedding books. 'The superstition used to be that if the bride has an older unmarried sister the sister has to dance barefoot at the wedding or she'll die an old maid.'

Mona Lisa sat up and took notice. 'That's a superstition we'll have to revive. She used to boss me about something rotten while we were kids.' The singer's face was lit by an evil grin. 'I suppose we couldn't stretch barefoot a bit?'

Alice was liking Mona Lisa more and more but she kept her face straight. 'That's up to you. If you cared to tell her that, by tradition, she had to dance topless, I might not contradict you. You could recruit a few pals to back you up.'

'Great. Though bare-arsed might be better.

Don't look so shocked, I'm only joking ... I think. I've been having second thoughts, it's probably less work all round if I get Juliana to mark up the table plan for you.'

'Fine. Remind her not to miss any tee-totallers or vegetarians or vegans or anyone who needs kosher food. And then,' Alice referred to her lists, 'you'll have to decide for yourselves who's going to speak; and we'll need a list for the toastmaster. What else?' She consulted her lists again. 'Instead of numbering the tables, we thought we might give them names out of Scottish history.'

'Bruce and Wallace, you mean?'

'And some of the inventors that people don't remember were Scots. Good pro-Brit propaganda.'

'Why not? And Burke and Hare?'

'As you say, why not?' said Alice. 'I know a firm who can make up little signs complete with potted biographies. At least that should give the guests a conversation-starter. And something else you might care to think about. Some of your guests will be camera nuts, but why not get a whole lot of those little throwaway cameras to distribute among the other guests so that they can photograph the proceedings and each other? Processing and printing are included, so they can either take them away or return them to us. Or would your magazine object? And you'd better put us in touch with whoever's making the video. If we don't coordinate our efforts we'll be falling over each other.'

The singer was showing signs of mental exhaustion. 'Leave those thoughts with me for the moment.'

'Right.' Alice looked at her watch. 'That's all we have time for. Sue Evans wants to meet us and agree menus.'

In the small hours of the following morning, Alice found herself wide awake. No arrangements had been discussed for receiving and putting on show the mass of wedding presents that was surely to be expected. There was a small ante-room with doors to the entrance hall, the ballroom and a passage leading to the chapel. There the jewellery was to be put on display. A table display of presents in the same room would surely be appropriate.

She switched on the bedside lamp. She habitually carried a notebook in which to jot down thoughts that must not be allowed to escape, but this was not in its customary place beside her bed. After a minute of sleep-drugged thought she recalled discussing certain points on the list with Sarah before settling down to sleep. She got out of bed and walked softly to Sarah's door. She tapped gently and then, hearing no reply, opened the door.

It was Sarah's habit to sleep with the curtains open and bright moonlight lay across the empty bed and Sarah's nightdress. Her clothes were tidily arranged on a chair. Wherever Sarah had gone, she had surely not gone there in the nude? The most likely answer had to be that she had donned something a little more exotic under her robe. Sarah, Alice knew, had invested some of her money in expensive lingerie that the designer had intended to be enjoyed rather than merely worn – and not just by the wearer.

Alice reclaimed her notebook and returned frowning to her own room. Sarah's manner towards Mr Dunwoodie had been friendly, occasionally flirtatious; but so it usually was with any older man. Alice had a feeling that any woman who lost the affection of her husband should have paid more attention to her job, but she loved her mother rather as one might love an over-affectionate puppy and she did not want to see her hurt. She hoped that they were being careful in more ways than one. She had no desire to see a divorce in the family, or be presented with a half-sibling on the wrong side of the blanket.

'Flowers,' said Alice. 'What flowers do you want on the tables and around the rooms? And for your bouquet?'

'What do you suggest?' Mona Lisa asked. 'My mind's gone blank.'

'That's not surprising. We're trying to squeeze into a short period what usually takes about six months. What colour is your dress?'

'Off-white. Sort of cream.'

'That's all right, then,' Alice said. 'Goes with anything. Let's think. Blue and pink are the only colours for the bride's dress, other than white, that have never been considered unlucky.'

'Is that right? Maybe that's where the pink-for-a-girl-and-blue-for-a-boy tradition started. I don't worry about these things but Craig's as superstitious as hell. You'd better make sure that none of the dining tables is named after the Thane of Cawdor. Let's stick with pink and blue. That would look well in the chapel too. What's in season?'

'I think the florists can supply just about anything from greenhouses or imported. Leave it with me and I'll see what they can suggest.'

As the Great Day came closer, Mona Lisa began to show signs of nerves. 'I do so want it all to go well,' she said at dinner. 'Most of what I do publicly is for the public, but this one is for me. Imagine the fun the tabloids could have if it all goes wrong.'

'It won't,' Sarah said. 'We're all working like maniacs to make sure that it doesn't.'

'But you can't control the weather. Suppose it pisses down and the marquee leaks. Had you thought of that? I'm going to try your telly for a long-range forecast.'

'Knowing doesn't change anything,' said the earl. 'We had the same marquee only a month ago and it was in tip-top condition then.'

'What's more,' Alice's father said, 'the world's three greatest liars are the politician, the priest and the weather forecaster.'

'And of the three,' said the earl, 'the forecaster is the only one who believes what he's telling you.'

'You're a pair of cynical old men,' said the singer, 'but you could be right.' She laid down her knife and fork and looked around the table. 'The other danger spot is the guests. Some of these characters have spent so long being told that they're the greatest that they've come to believe it. And publicity is absolute life's blood to them, whether it's good or bad. So bad behaviour becomes a habit. The reason I was so choosy about dates was to pick a time when as many as possible of the wildest ones are filming or on tour and can't come. That left one or two who I just plain didn't invite. The remainder are capable of behaving in a civilized manner, if pressed.'

'We'll have our usual security firm here,' the earl said. 'I notice that you don't travel with a bodyguard of your own.'

The singer laughed and winked at Alice. 'Lord no! Once you start to drag an entourage around with you, you just draw more attention to yourself and it just escalates.'

'You're not afraid of being kidnapped?' Sarah asked.

'I've thought about it, but I don't believe that the risk is worth disrupting my life for. I go around dressed as my drab little self and I'm very rarely recognized. I like it that way. I bought lessons from a bodyguard firm once and they taught me to recognize the danger signs and what evasive action to take. I never use my real name in my work, so I can live in what's officially my mother's house and none of the neighbours pays any attention to me. That way I can be myself.

'How did we get on to me? We were talking about the wedding and keeping the yahoos in line. As the acceptances come in, I thought that we might reply with a note telling them how happy I am that they can come, how to get here and, very tactfully, in among the positive points about facilities and so on, letting it be understood that mis-behaviour would be tolerated for about a second and a half and after that any culprits would find themselves on the way home. And about dress, making it clear that any photographs which are too far out won't make it into the media at all. I wouldn't even recognize half the guests in formal morning suits but I don't want anything too freaky. Some of the girls would turn up nude if it would get their picture in the papers, so I don't think we'll follow up your idea about the throwaway cameras, Alice. Could I ask that somebody help me with the wording? I want to put those messages across without coming over like a Victorian nanny and giving the media a good laugh at my expense.'

It was generally agreed that the earl was blessed with the greatest combination of tact and command of words. He accepted the duty with his usual grace.

Alice had adopted the habit of carrying Hugh around, supported on her left hip. 'You're going to slip a disc if you go on doing that,' Sarah told her.

'Nonsense!' Alice retorted. Sarah claimed that it was only poetic justice that an hour later, when they were together in Alice's bedroom, Alice felt a sudden stabbing pain in her lower back and had to hand Hugh over to Sarah in a hurry.

Alice had found, when the decision-making and ordering phase was over, that if not exactly at leisure at least she had enough free time to contemplate another visit home; but a sudden inability to move around except while carefully balancing her torso above her hips made her doubt the practicability of such a visit.

'Now you're being daft!' Sarah said. 'You could go and see your quack as part of the same trip. You can't even pick Hugh up at all in your present condition, so looking after him falls to us and the castle staff.'

'Exactly,' said Alice. 'So how could I

manage if I took him home?'

'You couldn't. So leave him with us. This is your chance to have a baby-free second honeymoon with Justin. Or possibly the third or fourth, I wouldn't know.'

This suggestion was generally endorsed. Hugh was a happy baby. He seldom cried and was usually ready to respond with a cheerful gurgle when spoken to. Mr Dunwoodie was pleased to have his only grandchild around. The earl had come to enjoy his walks around the garden with the pram, accompanied by Suzy and several of his own spaniels. Sarah and the castle staff regularly volunteered for nappy duty. The imminence of a wedding had brought a general broodiness into the air.

Alice bowed to the general will.

Next morning, she tried herself out in Sarah's MG and set off with a hard cushion strategically placed against the small of her back. She managed the journey without any great discomfort and extricated herself from the car with the aid of a heavy walking stick borrowed from the earl.

Justin and his staff were disappointed by Hugh's absence but they were properly sympathetic over Alice's back problem. Humph was restrained from offering too violent a welcome home. While she sorted the backlog of accounts and invoices, seated in the carefully adjusted typing chair, Colin even visited the jumble sale at a nearby church hall and came back with a Victorian lady's walking cane to replace the earl's weighty stick. Aided by this, Alice went to keep an appointment with her GP.

The doctor could only offer a prescription for painkillers and suggest a week of bed rest, neither of which was acceptable to Alice. However, the work of an engraver is hard on the back and Justin had had his own problems. That night, he introduced Alice to a set of exercises designed to straighten out the kinks in the most twisted spine. They had agreed that sex was out of the question, but he found the prospect of Alice, in a very short nightie, lying flat and repeatedly pulling her knees up towards her chin, highly erotic. His excitement communicated itself to Alice and their resolution weakened. Justin was intrigued to find the usually active Alice for once an entirely passive partner and Alice was quite charmed to have Justin proceeding very slowly and with care and consideration. The result was their most protracted and satisfactory coupling ever.

In the morning, Alice's back was improved; or else her mood was such that the pain seemed less obtrusive. Under her supervision, Justin carried out the cleaning and tidying that Alice had intended to undertake and then helped her tenderly into the MG. The vacant carrycot made a convenient receptacle for the several changes of clothing that she would require. The spell of unsettled weather that had brought Mona Lisa's fears to the boil had passed by. The August sunshine had returned so that the singer was now prophesying sunstroke or at best the guests appearing in her wedding photographs with peeling noses. Alice, however, if she ignored her improved but still aching back, was feeling good. Justin put the top down for her and she set off with the wind in her hair, knowing that she looked as good as she felt. A glamorous young woman with a sports car. Every yob's dream of delight. She had no desire to be approached by any of the men who, she thought, were casting appreciative glances at her, but it was pleasant to think it possible.

She drove at a moderate pace. More work and the ultimate challenge of the wedding itself were waiting for her. She would have travelled even more slowly to postpone reality and to prolong the pleasure of the drive, except that the road was twisting and not very wide and there was enough traffic to create a tailback whenever she dropped below fifty. Not far from the castle she entered a straight on which there was no oncoming traffic. She lifted her foot and signalled left. Several cars bustled past.

A mile further on, she turned in to one of the castle drives. This was not the main drive, which would have been approached from a different public road, but a narrower drive used by the family and by tradesmen's vans. Alice preferred the shorter route and the less formal approach to the castle.

Halfway along, she found her way blocked by a wide, red car which had stopped in the centre of the drive. She thought that she remembered it as having been one of the cars that had so recently overtaken her. The driver was walking back in her direction. Alice, made indulgent by her good mood, prepared to ask him whether he had lost his way.

While he was still ten paces away, he produced a large, blue-black semi-automatic pistol and pointed it at her head.

Alice's mind seemed to have stalled, but some part of it must still have been functioning. She had seen enough television to know the appropriate action and Mona Lisa's remarks about kidnapping had brought the subject to the front of her mind. She found that she had already slammed the car into reverse and taken off. Trees were streaming away from her, like a film running backwards. Rather than turn her head, she steered to keep the drive straight in front of her.

The man seemed nonplussed, uncertain whether to shoot or to run back to his own car. Instead of doing either, he began to pound in pursuit. There was no time to verbalize thoughts, but in a stream of mental pictures Alice recalled having been told that hitting a moving target with a handgun was strictly for experts. She hoped that the man was not expert and that her informant knew what he was talking about.

The engine was screaming. It was time for the next part of the stuntman's trick. She twisted the wheel to the right and trod on the brakes. She should have delayed for an instant before braking, but the presence of a ditch on each side of the drive dissuaded her. As a result the car, with all wheels locked, described only a partial turn and fetched up parked across the road with its engine stalled. With a ditch in front and another behind, completing the turn was going to take more time than she had available. She began to grab for the door handle, ready to run, but a renewed stab in her back reminded her that violent action was still beyond her.

He came pounding up. Evidently he was far from fit, because although he had only covered about forty yards he was breathing heavily and his face was scarlet. She had been driving with the offside window rolled down, which made it easy for him to push the pistol against her face. 'Don't you try anything like that again, lassie, or you're deid,' he panted. His accent was deep Glasgow.

No reply seemed to be called for. Alice could smell sweat and gun oil. At very close range, she was reassured to see that his finger was sensibly positioned outside the trigger guard, so at least he was unlikely to blow her head off as the result of a sneeze. But that reassurance was short-term. In the longer term, whatever he intended, the omens were not good.

The man recovered some of his breath. 'D'you ken who I am?'

Alice could have made a guess, but she

said, 'I've no idea.' To her own surprise, her voice sounded calm.

He grunted and set his jaw. 'I've a message from Jock Brora to your father. Tell your da that he has just two days to find fifty grand and turn it over to Jock. And just to be sure he remembers, see's your wean.'

The last few words, which Alice correctly interpreted as a demand to hand over her baby, made her blood boil. She thanked her lucky angel that she had left Hugh with his well-wishers at the castle. Whatever might happen to her would be preferable to surrendering her child to this monster. The two walking sticks were beside her left hand. Her fingers closed on the heavier of the two. Given half a chance...

She was allowed a whole chance. Without taking his eyes off her, the man was groping with his left hand in the back of the MG, where Alice had put the carrycot as being a more generous and convenient container for clothes and toiletries than a suitcase. The castle was more than adequately provided with cribs and bassinets. Suddenly, behind his back, a wood pigeon clattered out from among the trees. To anybody unversed in country noises, it could have been the sound of a man bursting out of the bushes. He turned, pointing the pistol. Without giving herself time to think, Alice brought the heavy stick up and over and down two-handed with all her might. Her back protested but she ignored it.

She aimed for the pistol, but the stick came down on his wrist, hard. The pistol spun in the air, hit the man's knee and rattled under the car without firing.

Incandescent with pain and fury, the man punched Alice backhanded over the right cheekbone. 'If the wean's not here, you'll do,' he said. He went down on his face and groped under the low car.

If the man had intended to stun her he had overestimated the power of his own punch. Alice saw momentary stars. She was hurt by the blow but the adrenaline was flowing and she was far from incapacitated. She considered starting the engine and jerking the car forward or back, but years of driving, even her comparatively few years, had ingrained a deep aversion to running over pedestrians. She threw the door open, intending to run. The pistol had gone further under the car than the man thought. He was flat on the ground and groping as far as he could into the shallow space. The door caught him in the small of the back and effectively jammed him. He kicked furiously but he was caught between the door and the tarmac and his sleeve was snagged beneath the car.

Between the threat and the blow, Alice was in a state of fury at least a match for the other's. She dropped the heavier stick back into the car and took up the lighter one as being more suited to her purpose. Quitting the car, she trod heavily on the man. She had stopped weighing consequences and her scruples did not extend this far.

'*You* were *going* to *take* my *baby*,' she cried. With the thin stick she belaboured the buttocks and thighs of the trapped man and she cursed him with all the venom of a mother whose child is threatened. He roared and struggled. Soon she was beginning to tire and she was running out of words of abuse, but she summoned the last of her strength. In the end, the stick broke. At about the same time his sleeve tore free and he began to inch out from under the door. Alice darted round the car. The pistol was lying beneath the car but in view. With the shortened remains of her stick, she fished it out and picked it up just as the man rose up on the other side of the car. Already his right hand was visibly swelling, he was sweating and dirty and one of his sleeves was hanging off.

Alice knew that there were certain steps to be taken with slides and safety catches before firing a pistol, but evidently the man had readied it for action because when she pointed the pistol at him he suddenly lost all his florid colour and turned to run.

Alice had no compunction about shooting the man in the back. He had threatened her and her child and he had punched her face. A remote corner of her mind began to rehearse a story to explain how she had come to feel that her life was threatened while her assailant was facing the other way. But it turned out that her informant had been correct about the difficulty of hitting a moving target with a handgun. Recoil jerked the pistol up and her first shot caused a visible disturbance in the branch of a tree beyond him and to his right. She lowered her aim and decided that she had pulled the pistol off-line when she snatched the trigger. The sound of the shot was less than she had expected but the recoil was more. She had plenty of time; the man's bruised muscles had slowed his run to a jog-trot. She adjusted her grip. Her second shot must have missed his head by a whisker, because she saw the back window of his car suddenly star just beyond his ear and he jinked to the left. She thought that he cried out but her ears were dulled by the sound of the shots. Her third shot again missed and she heard the whine of a ricochet. Then the man was at his car and inside. The car moved away with a shrilling from the tyres.

Alice kept on firing. She was beginning to enjoy herself. She had got her eye in and she could hear her shots striking the vehicle. Sometimes she could see the dent and hole made by the strike. One was where she thought the petrol tank should be, but the car did not obligingly explode into a fireball, as would have been the convention on TV. As the car drew further away, she had to raise her aim. Then the gun clicked instead of firing and she knew that it was empty. A moment later, the car rounded a bend and was gone.

The man might have been counting her shots. This seemed unlikely in the heat of the moment, but if he had been sufficiently clear-headed he might know that the magazine was unloaded, in which case he might return. Hastily, Alice dropped the pistol into the carrycot, gathered up the pieces of her walking stick with shaking hands, hopped into the car and set about turning it to face the castle. There was no trail of liquid on the tarmac, so she had not managed to hole his tank; otherwise, she might have dropped a match or the car's cigarette lighter and hoped that the resultant flames would over-take him.

By now, Alice was well acquainted with the geography of the castle grounds. At the bend where she had last glimpsed the other car, the driveway forked. The other car had turned left towards the front of the castle and the main drive, so Alice turned right. Her route emerged suddenly from the trees in front of the gateway in the wall, but the security guards were on duty, holding at bay one small but persistent woman reporter. Alice did not feel ready for people yet. She drove on, parallel to the wall, by way of the estate-workers' cottages, the airstrip and the stable yard, all the way round the enclosed grounds. She approached the spread of tarmac in front of the main door cautiously, but there was no sign of her recent antag-onist. Tyre marks springing from a puddle and some fresh rubber on the tarmac suggested that he had turned down the main drive at speed.

Reaction was coming over Alice in waves

of conflicting emotions. She was shaking. She was near tears but at the same time she wanted to howl with triumphant laughter. Fighting to bring her face under control, she rounded another corner of the castle and returned to the gateway. The two security men were still stalling the journalist but they recognized both Alice and the MG and opened the gate for her. She parked the MG as close as she could to the castle door, grabbed up the carrycot and slipped into the castle.

Something was different. A sound? A smell? Had she wet herself during the excitement? The answer came to her suddenly. Her back no longer hurt. Her exercise with the walking cane had proved to provide the perfect alternative medicine. Just what the chiropractor ordered, she told herself. With every step she felt both better and safer.

A short passage brought her to the lobby outside the offices. She could hear voices – calm and unruffled voices, suggesting that the pistol shots had been muffled by the trees and had not caused a stir at the castle. But she had no wish to be seen or for her voice to be heard outside her immediate coterie. She scuttled up the winding stair towards her bedroom.

At he head of the stair she almost ran into her father. 'I must speak to you,' she said. 'Where's Sarah?'

One glance was enough to show Mr Dunwoodie that his daughter was in a highly emotional state. Another female presence was very much to be desired. 'I'll fetch her,' he said.

Alice hurried into her bedroom and sat down hard on the bed. She jumped up again and washed her face in alternately hot and cold water until any sign of tears had gone. When her father returned with Sarah and an ice bag for the bruise on his daughter's face, she was sitting composedly on the bed again. 'Where's Hugh?' Alice asked.

'Tom's walking him in the garden,' Sarah said.

'Inside the wall?'

Mr Dunwoodie had settled down on the window seat. 'If you come to the window,' he said, 'you'll see them beside the putting green. What's this all about?'

'I was ambushed,' Alice said. Sarah drew in her breath, sharply. She put a comforting arm round Alice's shoulders. 'Don't worry,' Alice said. 'Your car's all right. Do we know a heavily built baldy with a blue chin and a button nose that looks like it's pulled the middle of his mouth up into a sneer?'

'Jock Brora,' Mr Dunwoodie said without hesitation.

'I thought it might be. He tried to pretend that he was only a messenger.' Clutching the ice bag to her face, Alice told the tale of her adventure in the castle's back drive. She tried to make a funny story out of it but her voice had a quaver and her listeners were in no doubt that she had been badly shaken. When she finished, the silence lasted long enough to seem oppressive.

'Thank God you left Hugh here,' Sarah said quietly.

'Those were exactly my sentiments,' Alice said. 'But why was he on his own?'

'The last word to reach me,' said Mr Dunwoodie, 'was that his associates didn't want to know him. Unless he scores in a big way very soon, he's in deep trouble. That could make him desperate, and being desperate could make him a dangerous ally to have around. But don't count on it staying that way. If he comes up with a good proposition he may be able to recruit some help.'

'Do we let the police know?' Alice asked. 'He shouldn't be hard to find, with his car peppered with bullet holes.'

Her father shook his head emphatically. 'No way! For one thing, we don't want to start anyone wondering what we're doing here. For the moment, Mona Lisa probably assumes that we're part of the castle's organization and the earl assumes that we're her agents. We want to keep it that way. For another, the police don't much like a lot of pistol shooting. All right, so you had good cause, but a plea of self-defence wouldn't wash if all the holes are in the back of his car. And for all you know, you hit him. He may be bleeding to death in some lay-by at this moment.' He picked the pistol out of the carrycot and studied it. 'A bullet from this could make a nasty mess of a man, especially if it had passed through sheet metal first. I'll wipe this off and dispose of it where it won't be found, ever. I think we just wait and hope that the police pick him up for having bullet holes in his car. He's not going to explain that he was trying a bit of kidnapping and extortion at the time. Unfortunately, the car was probably stolen and I expect it's been dumped by now.'

Alice remembered her father's assurance that Jock Brora would not seek revenge by harming Justin, but she was beginning to regret her assault on her would-be hijacker's person. Quite apart from indignity and physical pain, male pride would be involved; and in Alice's experience this was a very potent force. If Mr Brora was looking for means to exact revenge, he might well think of reprisals against her husband. She racked her brains for a way to protect Justin without letting him know that she had earlier fallen from grace and put their comfortable co-existence at risk.

For once, Fate played into her hands.

Preparations for the wedding had passed from the planning stage to the practical. The wines, nearly four thousand bottles of them, were already stored in a cool cellar. Other provisions were arriving. The marquee, in the form of a large mound of canvas under a protective tarpaulin and many poles, was on the terrace. Wedding presents also were rolling up. These ranged from the antique to state-of-the-art and from ornamental to functional but almost without exception they were valuable. Even Mr Dunwoodie's tones were hushed as he was shown each fresh consignment. Later the presents would be put out on show but for the moment they were locked away with Mona Lisa's jewellery.

The earl being at home, the whole of the small company dined together in his private dining room. Naturally the wedding was by now a major topic of conversation; but that evening the talk was drawn to the subject of wedding presents by the arrival of the groom's present to the bride. This was a necklace of matched diamonds and pearls which had once belonged to royalty, albeit only foreign royalty, and which, Alice estimated, must almost have matched in extravagance the whole cost of the wedding.

Mona Lisa was enraptured with the gift but pronounced it too grand to wear. Nevertheless she clasped it around her neck, though not before she had phoned a message to her insurers to hold it covered. It looked out of place against her plain dress, seeming to cry out for a princess's ball gown ... or a diva's wedding dress.

Miss Evans asked about the bride's present to the groom. Dinner had finished, although the company was still sitting at the table, enjoying coffee and the last of the earl's decanter of wine, so the singer left the room and returned with two gun cases. The two guns were passed carefully from hand to hand and the delicate engraving drew murmurs of admiration.

'Alice's husband did the work,' Mona Lisa said.

The earl caught Alice's eye. 'He's an engraver, is he? And a good one, I can see. I'll tell you a story. You see this cruet?' The question was rhetorical. In the private part of the castle, the furnishings were all antique and immaculate. The cruet, a handsome silver set dating, Alice thought, from the middle of the eighteenth century, sat in the middle of the table. She had already admired the engraving. 'Originally we had four complete sets, but one of the salt shakers vanished. Must've been a guest wanting a souvenir. We managed to match it for shape, so near that you'd never notice any difference – Laurie spotted one in a car-boot sale – but it's plain. I've been wanting to get somebody to engrave it to match the rest of the sets.'

A signal passed between Alice and Mona Lisa. 'I liked him when I met him,' said the singer. 'Do you think he'd accept an invitation to my wedding and do the work for Tom while he's here?'

Alice felt a flood of relief. 'I'm sure he'd jump at the chance,' she said. 'I think it's a lovely idea.'

'He wouldn't have to transport tons of

equipment?' the earl enquired.

'Heavens no! If you can provide him with a stout table to clamp his vice on to, the rest of what he needs could almost go in one pocket.'

'Ask him to come straight away.'

As soon as she could leave the table without giving offence, Alice phoned Justin and caught him at home. Justin admitted that he had nothing very urgent in hand. 'But,' he said, 'what would I be doing at a film star's wedding? I wouldn't know anybody.'

'You'd know me,' Alice pointed out. 'And Sarah and my dad. Also Mona Lisa. That should be enough for anybody. That blonde with the big tits who you so admire on the telly has accepted. And there will be hundreds of potential clients there, all admiring those lockplates.'

Justin promised to come the following morning as soon as he had briefed Colin and Dave. Alice was on tenterhooks until his car stopped in front of the portico. She hurried out to direct him round to the parking area on the terrace. Then she could breathe again. All thought of what might follow if Jock Brora were still to be on the warpath she pushed to the back of her mind.

It was now only three days to the wedding.

Ten

The ice bag had reduced the bruise on Alice's face to a point at which Sarah's clever hand with make-up could conceal it altogether. She felt less self-conscious about meeting Mona Lisa for another question and answer session.

'I thought you'd have a dozen bridesmaids, several flower girls and at least one pageboy,' Alice told the singer, 'not make do with a single measly bridesmaid.'

Mona Lisa made a mark on the guest list that they had been checking together, sat back and stretched. The two were working in the small sitting room that had been put at the singer's disposal. Alice guessed that it had originated as either a nursery or a sewing room. It was a peaceful haven in the castle, which was beginning to bustle. 'I really mean this marriage to work,' Mona Lisa said. 'We'd both have been quite happy to sneak off and do it somewhere private, but that only makes you enemies and gets the rumour-mongers working. On the other hand, I'm not going to have my wedding ceremony turned into a circus. I can't guard against one of the guests getting a rush of arrogance to the head and beating up a photographer or some such idiocy, but I'm doing everything in my power to make sure that if anything too silly happens it won't be my fault.' She sighed. 'We have to go through the motions. With this crowd you have to give it your best shot, but I don't have many girlfriends I could trust not to turn up stoned and stand on the hem of my dress or set fire to the bouquet lighting a spliff.'

'Your sister?' Alice suggested.

The singer laughed. 'You haven't met her yet. She's about the worst of the lot. Also she's about two feet taller than I am and much better looking.'

'You're exaggerating,' Alice said.

'Only a little bit. She's totally unsuitable on all three counts. Are these really the very best wines? I've seen higher-priced wines on wine lists.'

'Those are higher-priced because there are only a few bottles left in the world,' Alice said. Her father had expounded on the subject. 'We can try the Internet if you like and see if we can pick up some of those for special guests, but in the kind of quantities you need to satisfy this horde, these are the best on the market. Nobody can turn up their nose at them.'

'That's good. The unforgivable sin is to look cheap.' The singer's hair, usually neat, was tousled by running her fingers through it, as happened whenever she was perturbed by any problem. Like Justin's, her mood could sometimes be judged by her hair. 'And you daren't leave out anybody who's even half as important as he thinks he is. It doesn't do to make enemies in this business.'

'You're certainly not doing either of those.' Juliana Hogwood, the singer's secretary and factotum, was to remain at base and not join the wedding party until the wedding eve, but she had been busy. She had been entrusted with the task of purchasing gifts – 'favours' – for each of the guests. Hundreds of decorative bags had arrived by Securicor. Alice had peeped into several of them and the extravagance of the presents had struck her dumb; but Mona Lisa had not blinked at the cost.

The singer leaned back in her tapestry chair and stretched. 'That's the way it goes.

The reception's a public relations exercise but the ceremony itself is something very special just for us, for Craig and me.' She laughed again happily. 'You wouldn't believe how I love that man. The feminist in me rebels at the idea of being gift-wrapped but I go along with tradition.' She sobered suddenly and a rare frown creased her smooth forehead. 'I just hope that none of these bums goes too far over the top. I'll pay for any damages short of somebody burning the whole castle down, but I don't want to be in the position of having to make my peace with Tom. I like the old boy too much for that. Which reminds me. Make a note to tell Sue Evans that we need beds somewhere nearby for four extra security guards.'

'They've had big weddings here before,' Alice pointed out. 'Tom brought in his usual firm to keep out autograph hunters and unauthorized journalists.'

Mona Lisa sighed again. 'And so far they've done a great job. But my insurers insist on sending their own men. They're supposed to guard the jewels but they can watch the wedding presents at the same time and help look out for any trouble.'

'Trouble?' Alice said.

'You know what I mean. What I've been

telling you about. The sort of trouble people get up to when they've had too much money, not enough education and a gang of people telling them that whatever they do is by definition OK and then they get let loose with drugs and booze. Fights, damage, suicide, you name it, the kind of thing that happens when the nightclubs are closing up and sometimes even at first nights and award ceremonies. I've tried to leave the real troublemakers off the list and the borderline cases got a special version of the welcoming note that Tom and I cooked up together, hinting that I'm hiring a pair of thugs to beat up anybody who misbehaves...'

'You aren't, are you?'

'No, of course I'm not,' the singer said impatiently. 'But they don't know that. The real dickheads have given up thinking for themselves; they mostly believe anything they're told, just as long as it falls some-where within the bounds of their experi-ence. It just may keep them in line or not too far off it. Are we finished?'

Alice looked over the list. 'You're sure that these two share a bedroom?'

'Absolutely sure.'

Alice raised her eyebrows but made no comment. Certain other pairings were just within the bounds of credibility but the two actors in question were known for playing macho, he-man parts. Oh well! 'This is as far as we can go until we're sure that all the acceptances are in.'

Mona Lisa sighed dramatically. 'There are bound to be a few mannerless bastards who don't reply at all.'

'What if some of them turn up anyway?'

'I think I could get away with having the security guards throw them down those front steps and pretend afterwards that I didn't know anything about it.'

'And then pray that their replies hadn't got lost in the post,' Alice said. 'When we've got the list as final as it will go, we'll have to go over the seating plan again. But I think my father wants you now to go and help him sort out the transportation – who's important enough to you to be fetched by helicopter, who can be left to come by coach or limo from an airport and who'll turn up in their own transport. Tom says that any performers that he personally admires he'll fetch in his own plane. And several of your guests want to fly themselves in, so who's going to man the radio and make sure that they don't all try to land on Tom's airstrip at the same time?'

Mona Lisa went off, waving her hands in agitation while Alice went to finalize the details of the crèche that was being organized. Some of the guests seemed happy to leave their children behind but others, perhaps less age-conscious and with press photographers in mind, had insisted on their invitations being extended to include their offspring. The kitchen was being kept posted.

The pace accelerated but the major steps that Alice had viewed with some trepidation mostly passed with no more than the occasional minor hiccup. It was soon clear that the departure of Mrs Silver had not been the disaster that Alice had supposed. Miss Evans could not be trusted to take action unsupervised but Tom, Lord Brechin, the Earl of Angus, soon had a grasp of the systems and knew his way around Mrs Silver's files. He proved a tower of strength, but with the approach of the unveiling of a new supercar which was to take place at the castle the week after the wedding he was usually too busy to wheel Hugh around the gardens. Sarah also seemed to have become involved in preparations for the later event. Alice (who was wondering, with increasing agitation, what she would do when the wedding was over if Jock Brora was still on the rampage) had only to set forth with Hugh to be summoned to an urgent conference. The baby-walking duty was delegated to a minor minion from the castle staff who was forbidden to step outside the garden wall.

Justin arrived to join the advance party. His quiet good humour made exactly the right impression. The earl welcomed him with open arms and then set him to work in a small room between the hall and the offices. Alice and Justin were too busy to see much of each other by day but, encouraged by rich food and wines and the world's most comfortable bed, their nights were perfumed with love and romance.

The second group of security men arrived. Though their uniforms were similar to the others, even to the kilts, the two groups regarded each other with suspicion. Briefed by Tom, however, they collaborated sufficiently to sort the sheep from the goats among the visitors and tradesmen. The newcomers also stood guard over the ever-increasing hoard of valuables.

A handful of men appeared just when Alice thought that they had left it too late, and suddenly the dining room was darkened by the appearance of the marquee outside the windows. Another squad imported more tables and chairs and set out the double space. Florists followed on their heels and flowers, to Mona Lisa's colour scheme, appeared on the dining tables, in the ballroom and more lavishly in the chapel. The castle was being transformed and Alice was entranced, but Tom took it calmly. He had seen it all before.

The first arrival on the eve of the wedding was Juliana Hogwood, Mona Lisa's secretary and strong right hand. Alice had spoken to her several times on the phone and had a mental picture of a highly trained and educated businesswoman in a grey suit and sensible shoes with her hair in a French roll. She was not ready for Juliana, who turned out to be a fat and jolly negress dressed in iridescent colours, with an accent straight from Kensington.

A later arrival was Sam Munie, Mona Lisa's agent, who had been busy organizing her forthcoming tour. He was a thin and nervous-looking man, bald as an egg, having a swarthy complexion and a wrinkled suit. He took over the admission of the selected magazine photographers and a TV company who had reached a satisfactory deal. All others from the media were ruthlessly excluded; Juliana made sure that they were made aware that all revenue from pictures, interviews and video images would go to charity. That information earned Mona Lisa some respect but did nothing to stem their efforts to capture illicit pictures or fragments of news.

The bridegroom flew in, piloting his own plane, to a rapturous greeting from his fiancée who was still overcome by the lavishness of his present. ('Ask him if he kept the receipt,' Sarah said wickedly.) Craig Arthur was quite as handsome as his screen image, but he pleased Alice by being quiet and polite and accepting wealth as a simple fact of life. Alice herself was happily married, she told herself, and Justin was almost as goodlooking as Craig and just as sexy, but if the forthcoming marriage should happen not to take place she thought that the uncommitted Sarah should definitely step into the breach.

Sarah, however, was definitely casting her lures in another direction and, to judge from the exchange of flirtatious glances, Alice still suspected that the direction might be that of her father. Whether or not this assumption was correct, Alice knew that whatever was in the wind had passed the stage of flirtation. In the course of several visits to Sarah's bedroom she had come to notice that her friend was regularly wearing some of the exquisitely provocative underwear, which could only have been brought from Paris and which was clearly intended for special occasions and more than private adornment.

At what might well have been regarded as the last minute, the wedding presents were brought up and set out on tables in the anteroom between the hall and the ballroom. It was an opulent display of gold and silver, silks and lace, fine leather, precious and semi-precious stones and ivory of questionable legality. (Mona Lisa said, 'A toaster and a few pots and pans wouldn't have come amiss.') On the other side of the ante-room, Mona Lisa's collection of jewellery made a staggering spectacle on black velvet, in locked glass cases borrowed from the earl's family treasures. The severe little stone-walled room took on the appearance of an Aladdin's cave. A non-stop round-the-clock vigilance by the security guards was instituted.

The flood of guests began, by car and coach, by helicopter, air taxi or private plane. Many of the faces were already familiar to Alice but their owners generally seemed smaller than she had expected, less colourful and universally older. Singers of rock and pop and jazz and ballads. Virtuosi on keyboard or strings or percussion and a girl who played the euphonium in a dance band. Mona Lisa's words of warning had been heeded and, although the general style of dress tended towards the slightly colourful and eccentric, only one starlet stood out from among the others as offering too much intimate flesh to the cameras and was invited to change into something a little more modest or go home. Shrill greetings were exchanged. Old feuds were resurrected until somebody, usually Craig Arthur or his best man, moved in to separate the parties. Alice noticed that the greater stars were usually courteous and well behaved whereas a make-up artist and one of the stuntmen were openly rude to the staff. Observing the dress and manners of people constantly in the public eye, Alice realized that it was not necessary to be loud or half-naked in order to dominate the company or to exude sexuality.

Mona Lisa's family, comprising only her mother and the sister from New Zealand, arrived and mingled with the show-business guests. They were referred to and addressed by the staff, respectively, as Mrs and Miss Lisa.

Juliana, for all her gaudy appearance, was a monument of efficiency. She had absorbed the system instantly, apparently by osmosis. Each arrival was recognized, classified, presented with a glass of Champagne and a bag of favours – navy blue for the man and lilac for the ladies – and allocated to the proper bedroom in the castle or dispatched in one of a fleet of hire-cars to the appropriate hotel. Personal staff and visiting hairdressers were whisked away to B & Bs and returned as if by magic when required. The whole company was to assemble for dinner but a running bar and buffet was available meantime in the ballroom. There had been no need to import entertainers. The company was made up almost entirely from members of the entertainment industry and most were only too eager to perform. A self-appointed master of ceremonies was soon allocating slots to singers and groups.

As afternoon merged into evening, the pattern was established and order of a sort prevailed. Behaviour was, on the whole, passable. The castle staff was well able to cope. One or two guests had succumbed to alcohol or other substances and had to be put to bed. One who had decided that he could fight anybody in the castle found that he couldn't, but there was a nurse on hand to repair any damage.

Some of the more moderate guests happily paid the fee and enjoyed the guided tour of the whole castle. Of these, the stuntman and the make-up artist already mentioned slipped away from the last guided tour and were discovered to be copulating almost naked on the four-poster in the principal bedroom with the curtains closed. The tour guide, unnoticed, removed the large part of their clothing that he found on the floor, leaving the couple otherwise undisturbed. They had not made themselves popular with the castle staff, however. Word soon spread. Two doors were locked so that the pair, while trying to slip discreetly back to their own rooms, had to scamper by way of three stairs and five long corridors, none of them unoccupied at the time, to the accompaniment of a slow hand-clap. This event was later voted one of the high points of the entertainment.

Alice decided that she could leave her laboriously contrived programme of events to roll onward of its own accord. She retired towards her room with the intention of having a rest and a shower before transforming herself for dinner. Mona Lisa caught her on the landing and stopped her.

The usually imperturbable singer was showing signs of nerves. 'Is it going to be all right?' she asked Alice.

Alice was amazed that the question should be asked at all. 'It's going splendidly,' she said. 'Nothing's going to mar your big day. Relax and enjoy yourself.'

'I suppose so.' Mona Lisa was carrying a pale leather attaché case with dark leather corners; one of a set kept in the castle office for guests to borrow for carrying papers or files. She pushed it at Alice. 'Here you are. I'll leave you to return the case to the office.'

Alice opened the case and looked inside. There were four of the bags of favours, two navy blue and two lilac. She said, 'But,' and then came to a halt. It seemed immoral – more immoral than the original deception – to accept gifts from somebody whom they had set out to rob and had come to like.

'No buts,' said the singer. She lit up in a smile. 'You're guests. You've done more to make my wedding a happy occasion than any of those wackos downstairs. And anyway, we're several guests short. The airlines refused to carry the Bloom Brothers after some incident with a stewardess last time they flew, and Jenny Orton's in the Betty Ford Clinic again. These would be spare and I want you and the others to have them.'

'It's only just occurred to me that we haven't given you a wedding present,' Alice objected.

'My dear, you've given me the best present of all. You've organized a wedding that will be the talk of the profession for years,' Mona Lisa said, with more truth than she knew.

'If you're sure,' Alice said weakly.

In their room she found that the low evening sun was rousing Hugh for his late feed. Justin was scrubbing away the grime of a day's work on the earl's silverware. She gave him a navy-blue bag and opened one of the lilac packages for herself. Among some minor but expensive trivia was a small leather box holding a wristwatch bright with small stones that she assumed to be diamonds. A pair of earrings which she took to be costume jewellery later turned out also to be diamond.

'God!' she said. 'We can't accept these.'

Justin looked up from trying a Rolex watch on his wrist. 'I don't see why not,' he said. 'You've sweated blood to make her wedding a success and if it adds to her happiness to hand out rich presents, well, why shouldn't she? How much is she spending altogether?'

Alice had been wondering the same and had concluded that if it was Mona Lisa's intention to out-spend the other stars who had held extravagant weddings in Scottish castles, she was succeeding. 'At a guess, not far off three million.'

'There you are, then. This is a drop in the ocean to her. You know,' he added thoughtfully, 'I thought you were out of your mind when you dragged me through here, but I'm having a ball. A whole string of big names who'd been admiring the scenes on those guns have been coming in to watch me at work and I must have handed out twenty business cards. Jalique's husband wants me to engrave his wife's image on some gold pendants for Christmas presents.'

'You could do that,' Alice said.

'On my head. If this goes on, I'll need another assistant to fill in backgrounds. Mona Lisa says that if only she'd thought of it in time she'd have got me to engrave her profile on the backs of all these watches.'

Alice picked up her baby and sighed with happiness. It was going so well. And she felt safe within the castle walls, with so many security guards around. The future could look after itself.

There was many a sore and sleepy head in the morning. On the previous evening, an attempt had been made to separate the guests into the conventional stag and hen parties, but exuberance and sexual attraction had soon led to a remerging on the groups. Alice and Justin had been bemused at first by the sparkle of the after-dinner festivities, but after a while they found themselves sated with music and stand-up comedy. When a squeak over the baby alarm reminded them that Hugh would be expecting attention, they slipped away to their room. There they enjoyed quite as much pleasure as the revellers downstairs, but the sound of festivity was still filtering through the heavy fabric of the building when they fell into sleep.

If they slept a little late in the morning, most of the assembled company slept later although a few keep-fit enthusiasts were already jogging, playing golf or making use of horses from the castle's stable. Mr Dunwoodie, who had been feeling the lack of his customary exercise, was enjoying a ferocious game of tennis with an Irish tenor. It was hardly to be expected that the whole company would rise with regimental synchronization, so a running breakfast buffet would be available for much of the morning in the ballroom while the dining room and marquee were being readied for the major meal.

Alice donned her one really formal dress so that she could be ready for the wedding but available for any emergencies that might arise, but earlier work had paid off and the enterprise seemed to be running on oiled wheels. The cake had been delivered at dawn and, to keep it out of the way of the catering staff, was on show on a low table in the middle of the ante-room that also housed the presents and Mona Lisa's jewels. The cake was huge. Because of the number of guests to be served, it had five tiers instead of the more usual three and the lowermost certainly weighed more than the bride. The security men were warned that terrible retribution would be exacted if they picked at the icing before the cake had been cut.

Susan Evans had proved, as Justin phrased it, more of a wet fish than a ball of fire. Alice, noticing a reserve on the earl's part, suspected that the appointment was unlikely to be confirmed; but Miss Evans seemed able and eager to cope with such minutiae of management as checking that the bouquets and buttonholes had arrived. After breakfasting (but without sampling the freely available Champagne) Alice therefore snatched at her first period of genuine leisure for several days and took Hugh, Humph and Suzy for a walk in the walled garden. It was there that Juliana Hogwood found her.

Mona Lisa's factotum was visibly flustered. Her usual beaming smile was noticeably absent and her broad, black face was beaded with sweat. 'Mona wants to see you, urgently,' she said. 'She's in a tizzy.'

'Why me in particular?'

'You'll see.'

On the point of picking Hugh up, Alice remembered that she was still being careful of her back. 'All right,' she said. 'Will you wheel Hugh around for me until he falls asleep and then put him in my bedroom? And return the dogs to the kennels?' She hurried indoors, wondering what sin of omission she could possibly have committed.

Mona Lisa's bedroom was immediately above Alice's. The singer, already in her wedding dress, was seated at the dressing table, being attended by the hairdresser. To judge from the crumbs remaining on her tray, her appetite had been unimpaired but she was obviously distraught. Disturbing news must have reached her since she finished breakfast

She turned her head sharply on Alice's entry, seriously incommoding the hairdresser. 'Thank God!' she said. 'You've got to help me out.'

'What's wrong?'

'Della Dingle's supposed to be my bridesmaid, but she's appearing live in Salford. She was going to fly up this morning, with not a lot of time to spare, but she tripped over a cable and took a fall yesterday evening. She spent the night in hospital. They hoped that she'd only given her ankle a mild sprain but now it turns out that she's broken a bone. She's on the way up, but she's in a wheelchair.'

'And you need a replacement bridesmaid?'

'Yes. Will you do it?'

Alice had already begun a mental view of the available ladies but this took her aback. '*Me?* You've got to be out of your tiny mind!'

'If I am, it's with worry.'

'*Please* keep still,' said the hairdresser.

'Sorry. Listen, I've been going over and

over the guests in my mind, trying to think of somebody who could fit into the bridesmaid's dress, wouldn't look too ridiculous for words in it, won't be too hung-over to walk as far as the altar and who I could trust not to louse the whole thing up for laughs or out of spite. And I came up with you.'

Alice felt an immediate twinge of stage fright. 'I couldn't.'

'Why not? Craig's bought a humdinger of a necklace for the bridesmaid's present,' the singer said persuasively.

Alice had a sudden vision of being paired with the stout and hirsute leader of Mona Lisa's backing group. 'Who's the best man?' she asked.

'Jamieson Lang.'

Alice hesitated. Jamieson Lang was an actor of exceptionally rugged male beauty with a reputation which, over the years, had linked him with almost every actress in the western world. Alice felt a momentary prickle of lust. But no. She was a happily married and sexually satisfied woman, she reminded herself.

'With the baby alarm hidden in the bouquet?' she asked. 'Suppose it sounded off during the ceremony.'

'I see what you mean. Who, then?'

'What about Sarah?' It was the obvious answer and would serve the dual purposes of helping Mona Lisa and distracting Sarah from Mr Dunwoodie.

'Would she do it?'

Alice could guess what Sarah's first question would be. 'What's the bridesmaid's dress like?'

'Look for yourself. She can keep it afterwards.'

Alice looked. The wedding dress was far simpler and more elegant than the usual run of such garments. Its counterpart hung on the wardrobe door, safely shrouded in polythene. It was an equally simple and elegant match for the bridal gown, following the ancient tradition originally intended to confuse evil spirits as to which was the bride. 'She'll do it,' Alice said. 'All part of the service. I'll go and tell her.'

She found Sarah at last. Sarah was checking the stock of wines. 'Unless they all go mad,' she said, 'the stock will last out and she'll have a surplus to start housekeeping with.'

'That's good,' Alice said briskly. 'Now go and change again. You've just become the bridesmaid. I'll get somebody else to guard the wine and check it out to the caterers.'

As with Alice, Sarah's first reaction was horror at the thought of taking a starring role before so many star performers. To Alice's surprise, the prospect of being partnered with Jamieson Lang did not prove to be a clincher.

'I'm surprised at you,' Alice said. 'When we were at college, your sole criterion was that the boy didn't have spots. And now you turn down the ultimate male sex symbol.' Since the subject was open, it seemed to be a good occasion to air her prime concern. 'Are you having it off with my Dad?'

The idea seemed to be almost as abhorrent to Sarah. 'No I am bloody well not,' she said.

'Well, Mona Lisa says that the bridesmaid gets a splendid necklace in exchange for a few hours of being decorative and she can keep the dress. Does that swing it?'

'I suppose so,' Sarah said ungraciously. 'All right. I'll go and see whether the dress fits. You'll have to dash around and find me some shoes to match.'

Alice set off again. Juliana Hogwood was still wheeling Hugh round and round the walled garden and making chirruping noises. Alice herself returned the dogs to the castle kennels, posted Juliana in the passage between the store and the ballroom and made her promise to ensure that any wines drawn by the caterers were served to the guests instead of disappearing into the boots of the waiters' cars. She then dumped Hugh in her bedroom and spent nearly an hour touring bedrooms in search of a lady able and willing to lend shoes size seven, AA fitting, white or pale cream. In the end she had to settle for a pair of tennis shoes but, as she said several times to Sarah, who would know under a full-length dress?

Sue Evans had received the bouquets and buttonholes but had done nothing about distributing them. Alice had barely discovered this omission when she found another. Ushers had been chosen but nobody had briefed them on how to separate those who were to be admitted to the chapel from those who would follow the ceremony on the large screen that had been installed in the ballroom, nor what standard to apply to the bride's edict that anyone too eccentrically dressed was not to be allowed past the chapel door. She found Justin in serious discussion with a pair of potential clients, detached him with some difficulty and sent him to deal with the ushers and then to ensure that the groom and best man were properly dressed and in place, complete with ring, in good time.

Breathing deeply, she herself went round with the flowers. Most of the guests were well accustomed to making themselves presentable in unfamiliar venues. Some, who expected Alice to act as dresser, were briskly disabused. Mona Lisa had made up carefully and was wearing a modest selection of her favourite jewellery. Although looking beautiful enough to belong in a glass case she was showing signs of panic. Alice fetched three glasses of Champagne from the bar in the ballroom, which was already busy, gave one to the singer, another to Sarah and took one for herself. Sarah was slightly shorter than the original bridesmaid and the flat-heeled tennis shoes did nothing to correct the discrepancy, but Alice's feet were beginning to hurt, so it was no great hardship to go down on her knees with a mouthful of safety pins to adjust the hem of the bridesmaid's dress.

She had barely finished this task when there was a knock at the door. Mona Lisa lacked any male relatives to give her away, but the earl, who had long been one of her foremost fans, had agreed to escort her to the altar. He now put his head round the door to say that the groom was showing signs of impatience and that the keyboard player at the electronic organ had run out of imagination and was playing, for the second time, the theme music from *Titanic*, which, said the earl, was unusual and hopefully inappropriate.

At this point the bride and bridesmaid both showed signs of wanting to start the processes of hairdressing and make-up over again, but Alice was firm. With invective and threats, she drove the pair into the corridor, down the stairs and through the labyrinthine passages of the castle, bypassing the guests corralled in the ballroom to arrive at the chapel door. There she twitched the veil into its proper folds, tidied the bouquet, smoothed both dresses down and sent the trio on their way up the short aisle.

Wondering whether there was anybody left in the world other than herself and possibly Justin who could do anything for themselves, she collected another glass of Champagne from the ballroom. She then retreated to the ante-room and took up a position from which she could watch the proceedings on the enormous ballroom monitor screen but also be convenient to the main doors if some late or unexpected guest should make an appearance.

All seemed to be well. The music had been well chosen and was softly played. Mona Lisa had consulted Alice about the vows and Alice had applied a gentle polish by eradicating one tautology, an unfortunate dissonance and an unintentional *double entendre*. She had also contrived to correct a seriously split infinitive without falling into the trap of elegant pedantry. The resultant prose, relayed with evident sincerity in what one commentator would soon be referring to as 'the two sexiest voices in the English speaking world', silenced even the Champagne-fuelled chatter in the ballroom. The speaker system failed for an apparently accidental moment when the bride was required to answer to her full name. A faint breath of amusement came from the audience when it was mentioned that the bridegroom's real name was Arthur Dingle. That had been an open secret for years. Alice checked that the toastmaster was in place, ready to arrange the bridal party and muster the guests past them, past the official photographers and into the dining room.

She returned to the ante-room. The security guards had moved to the ballroom doorway, from which they could follow the proceedings while still keeping the jewels, the presents and the cake in view.

The wedding was rolling onward. Although it was a civil ceremony it had captured much of the reverence of a full church service.

At the very moment when the registrar was pronouncing the couple man and wife, there was an explosion in the ballroom followed by the crackle of shots. The ballroom filled with smoke. Somebody screamed.

Eleven

Panic was immediate and total. Smoke filtered from the ballroom into the hall and with it the first fugitives. Overhead sprinklers came on, dousing the company. Bells rang shrilly. From the ballroom came cries and sounds of people falling. Whether the first fallers had fallen because they were killed or injured or had simply tripped in the panic or skidded on the now slippery floor, Alice could not tell; but there could be no doubt that others were tripping over them in the smoke. The first few to emerge were dry, but then, as the sprinklers took effect, guests emerged wringing wet. To add to the confusion Suzy, Humph and four of the earl's spaniels, which had been left confined in the castle kennels, had escaped and now decided to join the fun by slithering around on the wet floor and barking furiously. The official photographers and the TV camera team retired to the dry entrance hall but continued recording. This was exclusive and it was *news*.

At such a time the mind may freeze, but Alice surprised herself by finding that she was still thinking lucidly. Whatever was happening was no accident but had been contrived. And she could only think of one possible motivation. She could hear the security guards trying to restore order; any attempt to assist might only add to the confusion. She darted across the entrance hall. The dining room, she noticed thankfully, was still dry. In the ballroom, she could see no sign of flames to explain the smoke and she assumed that if there had been any fire in the ballroom the sprinklers had already dealt with it. The big video screen was still functioning, which argued against an electrical origin for the alarm. It shone through an eddy in the murk, showing the tail end of the wedding ceremony, but the participants no longer seemed to have their whole minds on it. Alice looked for Justin among the chapel guests but he seemed to have vanished.

Turning, she almost bumped into Laurie. He was white and he looked confused. She planted herself in front of the bemused butler. 'It looks like a false alarm. Go and kill the sprinkler system before it floods the dining room. And stop those damn bells.'

Laurie brightened and hurried away, happy to have a direction.

Alice began to retrace her steps, but she moved cautiously. She had no intention of blundering into an all-out war.

As she crossed the entrance hall, to her relief the bells stopped dead. More guests were emerging into the garden end of the entrance hall, dragging wisps of smoke with them and coughing helplessly, but nobody showed signs of having been singed. Alice recognized one of the security men from the ante-room trying to restore order. Another helped an elderly man, a doyen of stand-up comedians, who had evidently fallen and was limping badly. Alice took over and helped him to a chair. The only blood on him came from a graze to his face and he assured her that he was otherwise unhurt. Alice left him to recover in his own time.

The security men seemed to have managed to evacuate the ballroom with only limited damage to the guests, but they must have left their posts in the ante-room and elsewhere in order to deal with whatever drama was occurring in and around the ballroom. Justin appeared, escorting an elderly actress who had fallen and grazed her knee. Alice urgently wanted him out of harm's way. She grabbed him. 'Go back to the bridal party,' she told him, 'and have them wait where they are until we find out what's going on. There's nothing they can do except add to the confusion. Go round by the terrace. I'll come and report shortly.'

Justin sensed that this would not be a good moment to assert his masculinity. 'Right.'

Alice helped the elderly actress to another chair. She was on the point of resuming her cautious dash to the ante-room when she heard the sound that took precedence over all others – the sound, from the monitor on her belt, of a baby screaming. This was almost unprecedented. Hugh had absolute confidence in his routine, the arrival of his next meal and somebody to bathe and change him and rock him to sleep. Such was his confidence that he rarely uttered more than a subdued wail, a polite reminder that attention was due. This was more desperate. It was the cry that he gave when something different and inexplicable was being inflicted on him, such as an injection. Heart in mouth, she swerved towards the passage.

At the bottom of the spiral stair she met a man in security-guard uniform, carrying

Hugh over his shoulder. The baby stopped crying as soon as he saw and recognized her familiar figure. Alice's first thought was to thank her stars that, when the fire alarms began to sound, somebody had thought to collect the one person incapable of making his own way out of doors. Then the thickset figure set bells ringing and her heart swooped down as she looked again at the small mouth in the blue jowl and the short upper lip under the button nose.

Alice tried to withdraw her offer of thanks to the stars. This was Jock Brora. He had slipped in under the guise of a security guard – helped, no doubt, by the fact that the men came from two different companies. Her second glance also picked out the razor in his right hand and the supporting bandage on the same wrist where she had hit it with the walking stick. Instinct demanded that she made a grab for her baby but Brora lifted the razor and put the edge against Hugh's neck. The baby, she saw, had calmed and was reaching for the pretty razor.

'You're too late,' she said hoarsely. 'The money's spent.'

'I ken that fine,' he ground out. 'You think I'm a gadgie? Tak' me to where her jewellery's on show. And if any bugger interferes, your wean gets a malky up his wee erse.' His voice and his hand were shaking.

Alice said no more. There was nothing to say. Hugh's skin was more valuable than all Mona Lisa's jewels. She hoped that the singer would see it that way and rather thought that she might. The greater concern was how to ensure that when Brora left he would leave Hugh behind, undamaged. In the man's overexcited state, he might take Hugh along as a hostage and then God knew what would be the end of it. She might have cause to regret her assault on his gun hand. She turned and led the way as slowly as she dared, giving herself time to think.

At the garden end of the entrance hall, disorder was replacing total confusion. Guests, coughing and limping, were moving in a trickle from the ballroom doors to the garden exit. Nobody looked in Alice's direction, towards the vacant frontage end of the hall. One of the security guards came out of the ballroom, wiping his eyes and coughing. 'Smoke grenade and a firework,' he said. 'Stupid fucking joker, whoever it was! Panic's over.' Somebody laughed.

Brora was giving such total concentration to the task in hand that he seemed unaware of the confusion at the other end of the long entrance hall. Alice led him into the ante-room. For the moment, they had the room to themselves. The presents were still on display. The wedding cake on its low table shone palely in the middle of the floor, ornate as the Taj Mahal. The glass case containing Mona Lisa's jewellery was unbroken but empty except for an assortment of jewellery boxes looking futile without their contents.

Alice stopped dead. 'Somebody's beaten you to it,' she said.

The natural sneer on Brora's face became a thunderous frown. 'This is where it was? Some bugger moved the stuff to safety? Where is it?'

Alice's mind had swept ahead. 'Was that your smoke and fireworks?' she demanded.

'What smoke and...?' His voice cracked. 'No it was bloody well not.'

'There you are. Somebody picked the one moment when everybody's attention would be on the wedding – just as you did – to create an incident that would be certain to draw the security guards out of here.'

'Who the hell?' Brora was looking ready to explode from the sheer pressure of mingled fury and panic inside him but he could see the logic in what Alice was saying.

Alice was about to enquire how the hell she was supposed to know a thing like that, when company began to arrive. Two security guards returned from the entrance hall. 'Stop!' Alice yelped. 'Do nothing. He has my baby. Don't let anybody come near.' The interruption had given her time for another part of her brain to work. 'Hold everything. Everybody freeze. I'm going to the office for a minute.'

Brora was in a mood to expect hostile intent all around. 'No way!' he said.

Alice was too hyped up on her own adrenaline, endorphins and mother instinct to be put off. 'If you want to know who beat you to the jewellery, wait here. I think I can find out. You have my baby, you think I'm going to start something?' She glared into the man's eye. His round face and insignificant chin suggested weakness and she could now see that he was beginning to doubt his own power over the situation. 'Keep him safe, you bastard, or I'll gut you with my fingernails.'

Leaving Jock Brora to think that over, she turned her back and walked quickly out and across the hall. Her knees were like rubber and there was a band of tension around her chest, but no sudden noises followed her from the ante-room. From the ballroom came the sudden sparks from a camera flash illuminating the smoke. A contract photographer was at work, quite unaware of the far greater news story happening a few yards away. By the time she reached the office, she knew exactly what to look for and was quite prepared to invent it whether or not her assumption was correct. One comprehensive sweep of the eyes was enough. She hurried along the hall again to the garden exit. Most of the guests were outside by now. The cars of guests and the limousine service had been brought to park on the terrace to her right, making an impressive and valuable display of luxury machines. There was one noticeable gap. She turned back to the scene in the ante-room. Less than a minute had passed and the stalemate was unchanged.

She tried to speak reasonably so that even the agitated Brora could take it in. 'The glass cases aren't broken,' she said. She went on, punching her points home one by one like physical blows. 'The one person I can think of who had keys to them was Susan Evans, the castle manager. I think she was due to be sacked anyway. She was supposed to be taking messages at her desk and she isn't. One of the attaché cases has gone from the office. And Sarah – the bridesmaid – kept a set of the keys to her car in there so that I could borrow it in emergencies, and they've gone too and her car isn't where she parked it.' As she spoke, her eyes were looking past Brora's left ear, drawn by a movement and meeting those of her father, arriving suddenly from the chapel. 'Like I said, you've been beaten to the punch.'

Brora looked at her through narrowed eyes. Alice saw that he was sweating and she remembered that, according to her father, he was in desperate need of money to settle a debt and save himself from a maiming or worse. He was in that frantic state in which whatever might save the bacon has to be the truth. 'You're a fly wee hen,' he said slowly. 'You could have made it a drill that her stuff would be moved somewhere safe at the first alarm. Or maybe you're pulling the wool.' He moved the razor so that it was an inch from the baby's face. Hugh had been gurgling cheerfully and trying to pull Brora's ear but now, sensing again that something was amiss, he let out a single whimper.

Mr Dunwoodie seemed to have taken some message from Alice's gaze, but was it the right one? Telepathy seemed to have failed her. She had meant him to tackle Brora from behind while she made a grab for her baby, but he had vanished, his place taken by another of the security guards, joining the other who was hesitating beside the doorway.

'For God's sake,' Alice said, 'do you think I let off a smoke grenade and a firecracker just in case you turned up?' While she spoke another figure had loomed in the doorway behind Brora's back. Alice glared into Brora's eyes to hold them but in her peripheral vision she recognized the big figure, even bulkier than her father, of Mr Palmer, the head man of the security team put in by the castle. Alice had not been impressed by Mr Palmer. He was disciplined, well trained and willing. He was strong. He was also, Alice told Sarah later, as thick as porridge and impetuous with it. But she was still sure that Brora intended to remove Hugh as a hostage when he left and there was nobody but Mr Palmer to rely on for swift action. She avoided looking in his direction. 'Do you think we're bloody psychic,' she asked Brora, 'to empty the glass case and hide the jewels away when we didn't know you were here? The first anyone knew of you being in the castle was when I met you at the bottom of the stairs.'

She had held Brora's attention long enough to allow Mr Palmer to pace silently up behind him. Now Mr Palmer made his move and there could be no doubt about his strength. He reached over Brora's shoulder and took the hand holding the razor in a grip that drew blood. It was the hand which Alice had swiped with the walking stick and Brora gave a brief scream of pain. With his other hand, Mr Palmer took Brora's chin and gave his head a fearsome twist to the side.

Even without meeting Mr Palmer's eye, Alice had been sure that he had been trying to convey a message to her. She only hoped that she had interpreted it correctly. As the security chief made his move, Alice leaped the two paces forward to catch her baby as he was dropped, only to find him beyond her reach. Mr Palmer's attack had caused Brora to spin round. At the same moment, surprise or pain or an attempt to recoil had caused him to throw up his one free arm, and with it Hugh.

The baby was jerked out of his grasp, miraculously missing the razor. His head nearly struck one of the ribs of the cross-vault overhead – nearly but not quite. Alice darted forward, desperate to catch Hugh before he came down from a height on to the stone floor or to hurl her own body underneath as a cushion to break his fall, but Mr Palmer's grip had swung Brora into her path and the two of them blocked her way for a vital instant. She swerved. She might still have been in time, but Humph had followed her into the ante-room. He yelped as Alice trod on him and she was brought to her knees. She twisted her neck and watched, dry-mouthed.

Hugh's trajectory seemed to continue forever in the slowest of motions. Alice had time to think that a baby's bones were flexible but surely not supple enough to withstand such a fall. Another security guard started forward from the doorway, but far too late.

Hugh was not unaccustomed to being tossed in the air. Justin had a theory that it would bolster his readiness for such sports as skydiving or bungee jumping. As Hugh descended, Alice had one frozen glimpse of his face. It registered fright but also curiosity, as if he were wondering what these strange events portended and who was going to catch him this time.

Then he landed. He came down squarely,

bottom first, on the uppermost tier of the wedding cake. The little silver Corinthian columns collapsed sideways and the first tier came down on the second. The Ionic columns broke and the second tier descended on the third. Doric columns at two levels were impacted into the rich cake. Icing flew wide and Alice saw her baby, the fruit of her loins and her hope of immortality, sitting amid the shattered remnants of Mona Lisa's wedding cake. He let out one long howl and then, finding himself unhurt, encased in food and the subject of universal attention, he subsided, looking, if anything, rather pleased with himself for mastering the power of flight and coming in to a safe touchdown.

Alice snatched him up. Cake crumbs, she told herself, would brush off. Once she had assured herself that he was truly undamaged, her first upsurge of relief became an explosion of fury. Brora was flat on the stone floor, his head turned to one side as if he was looking over his shoulder. Alice made for him.

'Don't touch him,' Mr Palmer said quickly. 'I've racked his neck for him. If he's moved it'll likely kill him or paralyse him for life.'

'Great!' Alice said through clenched teeth. Keeping careful hold on Hugh, she began to swing her foot.

Mr Palmer snatched her up with one arm around her waist and the other supporting Hugh. 'Nane o' that,' he said. 'Your da telled me whit was adae. I used whit they cry reasonable farrach, but gin the bugger dees I'll no hae ma sorras tae seek.'

His words stopped Alice's foot in mid-swing. Mr Palmer was right. No court would deem his action in rescuing Hugh from a razor-wielding gangster to have been excessive, but if Jock Brora died as a result of it then Mr Palmer might find himself caught up in the punitive processes of the law, which would be a poor reward for his prompt action. She sighed. Perhaps after all she would have to leave retribution in the hands of the drug barons who were after Brora's blood. She wished them luck and the patience to wait for him to come out of prison.

She drew her mind back from the trouble now resolved and thought quickly about the bigger picture. There would be a lot more thinking and work to be done and her blood sugar must be getting low. She picked a piece of icing sugar off her shoulder and popped it into her cheek.

Her cellphone was in a thin leather case attached to her belt beside the baby monitor. 'All right,' she said. 'I'll call an ambulance. Look after the bad bastard until it gets here; but if somebody looks like treading on him, don't get in the way.'

The beautifully scripted event had been transformed from a celebration into a rout and nobody was doing much to help. Alice found that her hands were still shaking and her jaw was clenched. In the let-down, she wanted nothing more than an excuse to slap somebody but she would have settled for a cup of tea and a good cry. She realized that the earl and Sarah were stuck with the bridal party and waiting for news. They were probably best kept out of the way until order was established. Sue Evans had gone and Mr Dunwoodie might be assumed to be in pursuit. With a bit of luck some born leader might have emerged and imposed a fresh control on the disruption, but she doubted it. From what she could see through the doorways, the whole throng was milling around, waiting to be given a lead.

For once, Hugh was an embarrassment. Juliana Hogwood had left the wine store to fend for itself and she was in the hall, wet and coughing but nevertheless managing to offer comfort to a tearful young pop singer whose dress, already skimpy, had been badly torn in the confusion, possibly by an opportunist male hand. Alice handed Juliana the baby with a few crisp instructions and thanked her lucky stars that nobody wanted to argue with her. That would have been the last straw. Sarah later assured her that when she was on the rampage the devil himself would have given way. Alice, who had always considered herself the mildest of pussycats, was amazed and disbelieving.

At least the weather remained calm and dry. The toastmaster was hovering uncertainly near the garden door. Alice got hold of him. 'Get all the guests out into the garden,' she said. 'Make sure that they all know that it was only a smoke grenade and a firecracker. There will be Champagne on the terrace. They can enter through the marquee when the meal's ready.'

The toastmaster nodded and hurried away, relieved to have a positive instruction, a function to fulfil and the authority to carry it out.

Some of the guests recognized Alice as a person who might know just what the *hell* was going on, but she slipped past them. She dived in through the opening in the marquee and found the head waiter wringing his hands. 'Gather up your men,' she said. 'Serve Champagne out on the terrace and go on serving it until further notice. If the Champagne runs out, serve spritzers – they won't notice by then. When you have time, see what you can salvage of the wedding cake. It's been sat on.' She switched her attention to Gordon, the footman. 'Gordon, get the damn dogs back into the kennels before they find the cake. Then move your doings to the entry to the marquee,' she told him. 'The guests will be coming in that way. Leave room for the bridal party.'

'Right, miss.'

In the dining room, she was relieved to see that, although some smoke had penetrated from the ballroom it had never triggered the sprinklers and was already almost clear. She closed the big doors to the ballroom. The ventilation system could do its work in there. She headed for the kitchen and found the head chef peering suspiciously over the servery counter. 'The panic's over. How long until you serve the meal?' she asked him.

'Half an hour. Maybe more.'

'Make it more. Give us an hour to sort

things out and for the smell of smoke to clear. Meantime, use any fans you can get hold of to push the smell of smoke out of the dining room and marquee and replace it with the smells of food. That should reassure people.'

He brightened up. 'Can do.'

In the ballroom, she paused while she looked around. What was the next most urgent task? The sprinklers had been cut off and the air conditioning had already reduced the smoke almost to an acceptable level. There were some scorch marks on the floor from the firecracker and the whole floor was awash. If it were left to soak, the beautifully polished boards would swell and lift, as had happened in her aunt's house following a burst pipe. The remains of the smoke grenade still lay in the middle of the floor. Some flowers had been overturned and were scattered soggily underfoot. On the other hand, one elderly male singer, famous for his capacity for alcohol, was still firmly planted at the bar, soaking wet but persevering. 'Champagne in the garden,' she told him firmly. She turned him in that direction and gave him a friendly push. 'Get changed into something dry,' she called after him. He hesitated, shrugged and changed direction towards the stairs. The video screen still showed the chapel and the nucleus of the wedding party waiting uncertainly for news.

Laurie, the butler, appeared, apparently from nowhere. She pointed. He nodded. That was enough discussion.

As far as she was concerned Jock Brora could remain as he was forever, preferably where she could take a kick at him whenever she passed; but she could hardly procrastinate much longer. She still had her cellphone in her hand. She keyed the code for the emergency services and requested an ambulance. Then she asked for attendance by the police. Without misrepresenting the truth, she made the request sound as far from urgent as she could.

Champagne was being ferried into the dining room, for pouring and onward transmission into the garden. She grabbed a tray, loaded it with brimming glasses and headed into the ante-room. Mr Palmer and two of his staff were fending off a small group of guests who had sensed that there was some drama in the ante-room and wanted to become involved. The men were also standing guard over Jock Brora, although it was obvious that the injured man was going nowhere under his own power. From the tearful groans, he was feeling very sorry for himself.

'I've told him,' Mr Palmer said, 'that if he moves a muscle he'll likely end up paralysed.' Alice raised her eyebrows at him and, out of the stricken man's field of vision, Palmer made a face and shook his head. Alice was beginning to like Mr Palmer.

The security men, now that the emergency had passed, were becoming preoccupied with the fact that they had let Mona Lisa's collection of jewellery be stolen from under their noses, the very disaster that they had been engaged to prevent. She was tempted to rub their noses in the mess, but Mr Palmer had saved Bruce from some terrible fate, though at the cost of a top-of-the-range wedding cake, so she was prepared to forgive. Whether the insurance company would be similarly forgiving was quite another matter. She gave the security men a glass apiece. Through the open doorway she could see that the garden end of the entrance hall had become a first-aid station where the few who had been slightly injured in the melee were being treated from the contents of the castle first-aid box by other security men and fellow guests. A rock singer with an unsurpassed reputation for rowdy behaviour was gently applying sticking plasters to the bride's sister, who had cut her bare feet on a broken Champagne flute. There was a steady procession of guests heading for their rooms and dry clothes, but the general mood seemed to be upbeat. Mona Lisa's wedding had at least proved *different*.

So much for the guests. Moving as briskly as she could without spilling her precious burden, she trotted along the corridor to another ante-room and the chapel. This was a bright and airy room, only demarked as religious by Norman-style windows and a white-clothed table which only needed brassware to be brought out from below to be transformed into an altar. The upholstered stacking chairs were no longer in their precise rows.

All the faces turned as she came in.

The keyboard player was still at work because the bridal party was still present and nobody had told him to stop. He was plodding his way through one of the Shostakovich Jazz Suites. Most of the chapel guests had fled into the garden at the first whiff of smoke or the sound of the alarm bell, but a few remained and were clustered round the bride and groom. The single video cameraman had stuck to his post and Alice saw that he had panned the camera to follow her entrance. Perhaps her words would reach the guests via a second monitor on the terrace and prevent the circulation and publication of wild rumours – not that anybody's imagination was likely to conjure up any rumour wilder than the truth.

Mona Lisa might well be glad that she was wearing a selected choice of her jewels, but unfortunately, due to a last-minute change of mind, not the groom's gift necklace. With her veil back, she was a beautiful bride but Sarah almost matched her for looks. Justin was striving to entertain the assistant registrar, a thin, grey-haired lady who looked as though she had seen it all before.

'Everything's more or less back on track,' Alice said. 'Have some Champagne and I'll explain.' She refused to raise her voice and talk above the noise produced by an electronic organ which was being played vigorously in church-organ mode. She took a glass to the keyboard player and told him that he could stop and rest his weary fingers. The silence was bubbling with curiosity. Her tray of glasses just went round those present, leaving two for herself. She had a feeling that she was earning them.

The earl raised his glass to the bride and groom. 'Now,' he said to Alice. 'I think that we've been amazingly patient in the circumstances, but there are reasonable limits. Do please fill us in.'

Twelve

Alice had been working out how to convey the facts, succinctly and without leaving room for any of the misunderstandings that seemed to be poised to add to the confusion. There was no doubt that the truth, or some version of it, would very shortly do the rounds, so there seemed to be little profit in trying to obscure any part of it.

'I have to tell you,' she said in the direction of Mona Lisa, 'that two different individuals latched on to the rather obvious fact that everybody's attention would be on you in the moment when you tied the knot, so that that would be the ideal time to make off with your jewellery. A known criminal got in dressed as a security guard and grabbed my baby as a hostage, to prevent the security guards getting in his way. Mr Palmer, the senior of the insurance company's security guards, dealt with him very firmly.

'That intruder couldn't have succeeded

anyway, because somebody else – Sue Evans, I'm quite sure – got in first and let off a smoke grenade and a firework in the ballroom to draw off the guards. The firework sounded exactly like shots and the smoke set off the alarms and sprinklers, so the ruse worked. To add to the pandemonium, she let the dogs out. She made off with the jewels ... in your car, I'm afraid, Sarah. My father seems to have gone after her. I've phoned for an ambulance and requested a police presence. The sprinklers were only set off in the ballroom, thank God!'

She paused. 'Why do you suspect Miss Evans?' the earl asked her.

'She had the keys to the glass cases, which aren't broken. She's vanished. And so has one of the attaché cases from the office. Sarah's car has also vanished and Miss Evans had access to the keys.'

Despite his dissatisfaction with her as an employee, the earl was reluctant to believe the worst of Sue Evans. He pursed his lips 'That isn't exactly the proverbial smoking gun.'

'If she proves innocent I'll apologize, but she seems to be the one person who isn't around any more.'

There was a silence while they digested the

story. Mona Lisa was the first to speak. 'Is little Hugh all right?' she asked.

Alice projected a warm look towards a woman who could put another's child before her own fabulous collection of jewellery. 'He's fine now,' she said. She took a sip of Champagne and realized for the first time how dry her mouth had become. 'Juliana's looking after him. I'm afraid your wedding cake had to break his fall, but I think the bottom tier's OK and I've told the head waiter to salvage as much as he can. It should go round everybody if it's sliced thin.'

'They can sleep with the crumbs under their pillows. But what's happening to the guests?' Mona Lisa asked. 'It must be pandemonium through there.'

'I'd better go and see what I can do,' said the earl.

'Before you rush off,' said Alice, 'you'd better hear the rest. Your butler has summoned the indoor staff to mop out the ballroom. I think they've caught it in time before the floor gets badly damaged. I sent your guests to have their Champagne on the terrace while the smoke clears and I put back lunch for half an hour. I suggest that you have the option of going to mingle with them now, or else wait here and then go and stand in the entrance to the marquee to do the kissing and handshaking bit.' She made eye contact with the earl and then the best man. 'I hope you don't mind that I've been bossy and handing out orders all over the place, but you were stuck here and there didn't seem to be anybody available and willing to take charge.'

'I can't say that I'm surprised at that. They were probably following the old navy motto – "If in danger or in doubt, Wave your arms and rush about." My dear,' said the earl, 'you seem to have done admirably. Do please rest on your laurels for the moment.' He turned to Mona Lisa. 'If Mrs Dennison is right – and I have every fear that she is – I can only say that I'm deeply sorry that an employee of mine has robbed you and upset your wedding. I knew that she was incompetent but I thought at least that she was honest. I'll do what I can to make amends. Now I must go and see what other damage has been done. I'll catch up with you as soon as I can.'

'Is Sue Evans a competent driver?' Sarah asked anxiously.

The earl captured one of Sarah's hands. Alice saw him give it a comforting squeeze.

'One of the best,' he said. 'I made sure of that before I took her on because she had to drive my cars now and again, and it's one area I couldn't fault her on. So don't worry too much about your car.' He patted the hand, released it and left the chapel at a brisk pace.

Alice subsided on to one of the chairs, lifted her heels out of her shoes and let peace and quiet settle over her like a warm blanket. She seemed to have been on her feet all day and in her best and least comfortable shoes. She finished the first of her two glasses of Champagne and started the other. 'Nobody else was badly hurt,' she said. 'There were some falls in the initial panic but people are giving each other first aid and getting into dry clothes.'

'Let Tom see to it,' Mona Lisa said. 'You've done enough, and done it very well.' She looked affectionately up at her groom and then at the best man. 'I suggest we linger here, have our drink and wait. I don't fancy mingling with the crowd, with everybody wanting to ask what happened and what's happening now.'

'That's for sure,' Craig Arthur said in his deeply thrilling voice. 'Specially as those who were in the ballroom probably know more about it than we do.'

The best man agreed. Sarah took a seat beside Alice. The lingering guests were down to a couple. The others, Alice thought, would have rushed off to spread the latest news. 'Is there anything we can do?' the man asked. His accent was American. Alice gathered that they were relatives of the bridegroom.

'You could send someone along with more drinks,' said the best man. 'And maybe some snacks. Well, I get hungry,' he added defensively.

'And tell somebody to come and give warning when lunch is getting near,' Alice said. 'Or perhaps I'll do that. I'll have to go in a minute and help cope with the ambulance and the police. Do you have a list of your jewellery?'

'Juliana has it,' said the singer. 'She won't have it with her, but her memory is out of this world. And she knows which pieces I've got on now. Have her sit in with you. Well, at least,' she added with satisfaction, 'this is one piece of excitement that Madonna didn't have at her wedding.'

Alice had already gathered that there was a trace of bitter rivalry between the two singers. 'Who's Madonna?' she asked.

Mona Lisa smiled. 'You're my kind of person. I like your way of thinking.'

Alice pushed her heels back into her shoes, pulled herself to her feet and left the chapel. She paused in the passage to key her father's mobile number on her own cellphone, but the service could not make a connection. Nothing had changed in the ante-room except that the remains of the wedding cake had been removed. Mr Palmer placed himself between her and the still-recumbent Jock Brora in case she still felt like taking a kick at him. The entrance hall seemed to have been cleared of casualties. Through the glass front doors she could see several of the security men keeping at bay some lurking journalists who had divined that news was breaking. The earl seemed to have become bogged down among importunate guests.

Alice detoured through the ballroom, where several ladies in overalls were bustling about to good effect with mops and buckets, and looked into the dining room. The smell of smoke had almost cleared but one of the castle servants was going around with an air freshener. The supply of Champagne was flowing steadily through to the terrace. The head waiter returned from the kitchen to say that all would be ready to serve the meal in half an hour's time.

'How long will it take to seat this crowd?' Alice asked.

The head waiter shrugged. 'Fifteen minutes.'

'In ten minutes, send somebody with drinks and instructions to bring the bridal party up to the marquee to greet the guests as they enter. When they're in place, tell the toastmaster to get on with it. Got it?'

The head waiter smiled and bowed. 'Perfectly, Madam.'

The mobile phone on her belt began to play its little tune. There was a small toilet off the entrance hall and Alice slipped inside. The call was from her father. 'At bloody last,' she said. 'I've been trying to reach you.'

'I couldn't have heard you anyway in the noise that chopper makes.'

Alice breathed a sigh of relief. She had noted the absence of the stand-by helicopter. Her sole fear had been that Sue Evans might have hijacked the helicopter, leaving her father with the hopeless task of trying to follow it from the ground. 'So where are you?' she asked.

He ignored the question. 'Is Hugh all right?'

'He's fine. Where are you?'

'Have you spoken to the police yet?'

'Only to request that they attend.'

'That's fine. You can throw them Jock Brora to keep them busy. Tell them about the missing jewellery. You can say that she seems to be heading towards Turnhouse Airport.'

The call terminated suddenly. Alice emerged into the hall and found the earl there, looking distracted. He pulled her into the passage leading to the offices. 'That bloody woman!' he said. 'It's bad enough having my clients robbed by my employees. But I've just been on the phone to my bank. She cleaned out the castle account.' His face was grey.

'Is it very bad?' Alice asked.

'Around three hundred thousand, and most of it due to be paid out to hotels and suppliers. And it falls outside the terms of my insurance. Just when we were back in the black!'

'That's bad.' Alice moved to one side to see through the glass doors and down the main drive. 'There's a police car arriving. Do you want to see them first?'

'I ought to, but I have a hundred other things screaming for my attention first.

Would you give them the bare facts and let me know when I'm needed to fill in the details?'

'Of course,' Alice said.

The earl hurried between the scattered guests. One man was still receiving attention to a hand, cut when he fell on a broken glass, from another rock singer known more for bad behaviour than for musical talent. Several were soaking wet but too deeply engaged in ardent discussion of the events, insofar as the facts were known, to go and change. Others were heading for the stairs and their bedrooms; some were returning, dry, from aloft. But there was a growing huddle of the guests who had been boarded out in nearby hotels.

Justin appeared in front of her. His hired morning suit was rumpled and marked with what looked like cigar ash. Worse, his hair was ruffled, a sure sign of mental disturbance. Alice had an uneasy feeling that she could guess what he was going to say.

She was right. 'Alice,' Justin said. 'Mona Lisa was talking to me while we were waiting for news. She commented how lucky the earl was to have you on his staff. But Tom already said that you were working for Mona Lisa. What the hell's going on?'

Alice experienced a sinking feeling as her old, half-forgotten fears came flooding back. Flouting man-made laws was acceptable and might be considered fair game, but breaking her promise to Justin had been to invite disaster. Several glasses of Champagne seemed to have dulled her wits but she recovered them, she thought, with admirable speed. 'Our role was an entrepreneurial one,' she explained. 'Both clients are happy. But I can't talk just now.' She looked frantically around for a suitable distraction and found one.

Of those guests who had suffered under the sprinklers, some had only to climb the stairs to find dry clothes and towels. Others, she could see, had borrowed not always suitable changes of clothes from friends with rooms in the castle. But there were some, obviously unaccustomed to having to make arrangements for themselves, who were clustered vaguely by the back door, waiting for help to materialize. The security men on door duty could not be spared and anyway would not be competent for the job. Laurie, the butler, was the only person in sight with any claim to an official position. Alice turned away from her husband and button-holed the butler. 'Mr Laurie,' she said rapidly, 'you've been brilliant so far. I know that this isn't strictly your department, but none of the regular transport is still out on the terrace and some of the guests need to go back to their hotels and change. At the same time, the hairdressers had better be fetched back here. And,' she added, suddenly remembering, 'those guests will need to be fetched back quickly to join the meal. Can you call taxis? My husband can take charge of the timing.'

Laurie smiled benignly. 'Leave it with us, miss. This way, ladies and gentlemen.'

Miraculously, the hall began to empty. Alice began to feel that order might some day be fully restored. A small police car had come to rest before the portico and two young-looking, uniformed constables were climbing the steps. Perhaps this would signal the point at which the official machine might steamroller events back into smoothly disciplined form. Or perhaps not.

Alice went to meet them. 'Would you come this way, please?' she said.

The two constables stood still. Evidently the habit of resisting any suggestion from the public was deeply ingrained. One of them produced the traditional notebook. He seemed to be slightly the older if only by virtue of being slightly taller. His uniform was very clean and smartly pressed but his prominent nose was disfigured by a scarlet pimple. 'And you are?' he enquired.

'I'm Mrs Dennison.'

'Address?'

'For the moment, my address is here. Now, if you will please—'

The constable smiled in a superior manner that made Alice want to slap his face. 'All in good time, miss.' At some misguided school he had been invested with a synthetic posh accent and he was evidently proud of it. 'We had a call to say that there was trouble here. I understand that there is some sort of show-business wedding going on, so I can hardly say that trouble is surprising. On the other hand, I understand that the earl assured my superiors that arrangements for security were well in hand. So what is the trouble?'

Alice became aware of a sensation, not unfamiliar from her earlier dealings with the police, of trying to run in treacle. She hesitated for a moment, choosing her words and making substitutions for the ruder ones. 'I am trying to tell you,' she said slowly and distinctly, 'and I can tell you better in the appropriate place and where we can't be overheard by reporters. I am going to walk there now and if you want to hear what I have to say you can follow me. Otherwise you can find out for yourselves.' She refrained from spelling out their alternatives in any more outrageous detail. The two security men on the main doors grinned at her behind the policemen's backs.

She turned on her heel and walked. Reluctant footsteps told her that they were following. She led them into the ante-room.

The senior constable hovered over Jock Brora. 'What happened to this man?'

Alice decided that cold irony would be more effective than the eruption that was boiling up in her. 'That,' she said, 'is an important part of what I have been trying to tell you for several minutes. If you wish to proceed by question and answer, please say so and then I'll tell you what questions to ask. Otherwise we'll be here for a week.' The constable seemed to be struck dumb at last. Alice resumed. 'As you ought to know, we're in the throes of a major wedding. Craig Arthur, the film star, is marrying Mona Lisa.' She pointed to the prone figure of Jock Brora. 'This man,' she said, 'decided that the marriage service would be the perfect time for a robbery. He got into the castle disguised as a security officer and took my baby as a hostage at knifepoint, intending to make off with the very valuable jewellery collection belonging to the bride. Mona Lisa, you understand? This man was injured in the process of being disarmed and my baby being recovered unhurt. An ambulance has been summoned. These gentlemen can confirm.'

Mr Palmer and the other security guard made affirmatory noises. Jock Brora began to protest but fell suddenly silent. Alice guessed that he had realized he would be safer in custody than running around loose.

The two constables were struggling to be seen in full command of a difficult situation. 'And where would this jewellery be now?' the taller one enquired.

'We don't know,' Alice said. 'He was beaten to the punch, we believe, by a castle employee, a Miss Evans, who had already made off with it from these showcases and had also embezzled a large sum of money from the earl. In the process, she drew off the security guards by letting off a smoke bomb which in turn triggered the sprinklers in the ballroom where most of the guests remained during the ceremony, so you'll understand that things have been more than a bit confused. She also pinched the brides-maid's car to leave in. My father set off in pursuit and he phoned a minute ago. It was a bad line but I think he said that she seem-ed to be heading in the direction of Turn-house Airport, Edinburgh.'

The other constable – even to Alice he seemed absurdly young – had produced a similar notebook and a carefully sharpened pencil, but he ceased writing almost im-mediately. 'This is too heavy for us,' his senior told him. 'You stay here. I'll call in from the car.'

Alice saw movements in the hall. 'The ambulance has arrived,' she said.

The taller constable managed to retain his professional aplomb. 'Stay with the injured man,' he told his colleague. 'One of us will have to go with him. I'll radio for instruc-tions. Don't let the ambulance leave until we've got them. Or anybody else.' He hur-ried importantly away. Alice thought that his back looked relieved at having delegated the more contentious part of the job.

Two paramedics arrived with a stretcher and began to fuss over Jock Brora. One went back to the ambulance for a neck brace.

'I'm not needed here for the moment,' Alice said.

'Stay where you are, please, miss,' said the remaining constable uncertainly. He was sandy-haired, fair-skinned and freckled and Alice thought that he could have been typecast as the stereotypical *boy next door.* 'You heard my partner. Nobody is to leave.'

Alice took a deep breath. She had had enough and more than enough of doing everybody's thinking for them. She lost her cool but retained her mastery of words. What she wanted most in the world was to sit down with a cup of tea, or at a pinch Champagne would do, and kick off her shoes. On a previous occasion she had suffered and accepted some pushing around from the police, but this time she held the moral high ground. She assumed the expression that she imagined a duchess might adopt when confronted by an impertinent servant.

'May I point out to you,' she said coldly, 'if you have not yet perceived it for yourself, that the identities of both guilty parties are known and that you have one of them here and the other is already far away. Also that there is a major wedding in train and many of the guests were soaked by the sprinklers and their transportation to and from their hotels to change their clothes has already begun. That makes it rather too late to try to keep everybody here. Furthermore, these are mostly celebrities and some of them must be millionaires many times over. If your chief constable has a favourite singer, comedian or film star, he or she will almost certainly be here today. Are you really going to take it on yourself to keep them standing around, probably in wet clothes, and make them miss the meal and speeches at what will almost certainly prove to be the wedding of the decade? If you do, who do you think will get the blame? Or are you going to think for yourself?'

The constable suddenly became human. 'Between you and me, Mrs Dennison,' he said, 'I thought my mate was sticking his neck out.' He turned away and became very interested in the ministration of the paramedics, making it clear that, while he would not take it on himself to contradict his senior, he had no intention of trying to enforce the latter's edict. He was learning an early and valuable lesson in keeping his nose clean while watching his back.

Alice turned on her heel and left the anteroom. First she made a rapid circular tour. The number of journalists besieging the front doors seemed to have increased but the security men were coping. No doubt the wall enclosing the grounds would soon be scaled and after that it would become impossible to keep the marquee secure. Too bad! The guests might get the publicity they no doubt craved. The official photographers had obtained exclusive shots of the initial upheaval, so no doubt the show-business charity would get its benefit. The ballroom looked clean and was drying out rapidly. The dining room was immaculate and the first guests were already congratulating the bridegroom, wishing the bride every happiness and being directed to their seats.

On the terrace, most of the guests seemed to be in possession of a fairly accurate version of the facts. Alice gathered that her report to the bridal party had reached them via the CCTV or else that the guests who had remained in the chapel to hear her report to the wedding party must have spread the tidings. The Champagne was holding out. The last of the wet, hotel-bound guests were being shepherded into a minibus by Laurie while Justin made entries in the book which he usually reserved for sketches of engravings. Bringing back the guests, some of whom would be impatient to rejoin the festivities while others would wish to spend time on their appearances, was going to be a logistical nightmare. Alice decided to leave them to it.

Juliana Hogwood loomed up, dry, showing her very white teeth in a smile and still lugging a happy Hugh with her. 'Bless you!' Alice said. 'Cope a little longer if you can. Listen. Mona Lisa's jewels have been lifted. The police will want a list but a rough value would probably do for the moment.'

Mona Lisa's henchwoman said, 'Wow!' She looked up at the sky for a moment and then glanced across at the bridal party. She wrinkled her dark brow for a moment in an effort of memory. 'Insured value,' she said slowly, 'less what she's wearing today, roughly a million and three-quarters. I'll give it precisely when I get my hands on my files.'

'That'll do for the moment,' said Alice. 'Keep Hugh a little longer, please.'

She could see, across the terrace in the entrance to the marquee, an earnest discussion within the bridal party. She made faces intended to convey a demand for back-up. Sarah exchanged a few words with the earl, spoke briefly to Mona Lisa and slipped away. Alice met her at the doorway of the hall.

'Let's head for the office,' Sarah said. 'Tom

wants me to look into what the Evans woman got away with and tell the police all about it. We can't both get away and leave bride, groom and best man to cope alone.'

'But why you and not his noble self?' Alice asked.

'Because I was doing most of the book-keeping from the time when it became obvious that Susan Blasted Evans was only pretending to cope. And, between you and me, I don't think that Tom's very happy with financial management things. He's very good at shaking hands and keeping guests jolly, but when it comes to money and computers you've got to keep it simple or he tends to boggle at the edges. Telephone banking's a closed book to him. Anyway, the bridesmaid doesn't have to do anything just now but he has a pivotal role as the bride's substitute father.'

Alice looked up at the ceiling in amazement. Sarah had spent several years living by her wits. She was, Alice knew, a competent actress. But that she could induce a member of the aristocracy to entrust her with his bank details beggared belief.

Sarah picked up the hem of the dress, revealing the tennis shoes beneath. As they crossed the hall, they saw that the stretcher was being removed to the waiting ambulance. The taller of the two constables went with it. The other looked at Alice and opened his mouth but she shook her head and he shut it again. She smiled a secret smile and wished that she had learned the knack of intimidating police officers years earlier.

At the office door, Sarah paused. 'I suppose I couldn't go and change into something sensible?' she suggested. 'I'm terrified that I'm going to sit on a chocolate biscuit or get this dress peed on by Hugh.'

Alice pretended to be deeply shocked. 'No way! You have to rejoin the wedding party, have your health drunk and then sleep with the best man.'

'Huh! Chance would be a fine thing.'

'I bet. For you or for him?' Alice asked, laughing.

'For either of us. He's set his sights on one of the pop starlets and I ... I have my own fish to fry.'

Alice stopped laughing and decided that the subject would be best avoided. If there were any scandal about to touch her father, she would prefer to remain unaware of it. 'Oh? Anyway,' she said, 'you look just great.'

'I look like a Barbie doll and if I sit down in this dress I'll change its shape forever.'

This turn of the discussion had reminded Alice of her current worry. 'Justin's beginning to ask awkward questions,' she said. 'Can you lend me something really, exquisitely captivating? I'm talking about something so provocative as to be verging on the illegal? Something guaranteed to keep a husband's mind incapable of rational thought or your money back.'

'Certainly I can,' Sarah said, 'but I'm wearing the best of it. I'll do a swap with you later.'

Alice's first act on entering the office was to put the kettle on. Then she sat down, kicked her shoes off and surrendered to the bliss of not having to think.

'I suppose this phone's all right,' Sarah said. 'This subject's a bit sensitive. But Tom had the castle and lines checked for bugging late yesterday, in case any of those journalists were trying to get their stories that way.' She began tapping codes into the telephone and then speaking but Alice let it flow over her head. The kettle boiled and she made tea.

After a minute or two, Sarah finished her note-taking, disconnected and accepted a steaming cup. She was stretched out inelegantly in an office chair in order not to 'seat' the bridesmaid's dress. 'She seems to have been planning this for days,' Sarah said. 'She was drawing out sums in cash as fast as they were paid in. More than a quarter of a million in all from the castle's current account and the cash limit on the castle's three credit cards. Rather than miss any crumbs, she also cashed in Tom's premium bonds. She converted the lot into large denomination American banknotes and other portable currency. Tom will not be a happy bunny.'

'He isn't. But I'm sure you'll be able to think of something to soften the blow.'

Before Sarah could reply the phone rang and she picked it up, listened for a moment and then handed it to Alice. 'It's your dad.'

'About time,' Alice said into the phone. 'I've been waiting with my mobile near my hand, wanting to know what to tell the cops.'

'And I've been trying to get through the old-fashioned way, because what I have to say is not for bouncing off satellites. I'm at Dyce Airport. You won't believe this—'

'I'll believe it,' Alice said. She was not going to let her father score points off her unnecessarily. She gestured to Sarah to pick up the extension. 'I saw that one of the attaché cases had vanished from the office and guessed that she'd pinched it to contain the jewellery and most of the contents of Tom's piggy bank, so when I saw that a matching one had disappeared I could guess who took it and why.'

'That's my clever little girl,' Mr Dunwoodie said. He paused. Alice thought that he might be waiting for her to throw a tantrum at the form of address. 'As you surmise,' he resumed, 'I managed a substitution. I thought at first that it would be impossible, because she knows my face and I couldn't see any suitably crafty-looking character to bribe. I did not want to invoke the airport police.

'She was hanging tightly on to the case and I was devising more and more unlikely scenarios for getting it away from her, but in the end she made it easy. She put the case down while she bought a cup of coffee, I emerged from behind a group of asylum seekers and swapped them over and I was out of sight again before she put her purse away. I thought that I might have to run for it or explain myself, but it seemed worth the risk. There was an announcement coming over the loudspeakers at the time and everyone was looking up at the monitors. The question is, where do we meet?'

Alice had hardly begun to digest the question when Sarah grabbed the phone and spoke. 'You come right back here,' she said firmly, 'or I'll make a full statement to the fuzz. Listen. We made thirty-eight grand on our mark-up on the wines, helicopters, limos and the castle booking. Mona Lisa was talking about a reward for the jewels and I can promise one on the money. And you can have it all between you. I don't want any. You can cut me out altogether. Call it Alice's share from earlier, which she never got.'

There was a long pause. 'I'm on my way back,' Mr Dunwoodie said. Even over the phone line, Alice could hear the resignation in his voice.

They disconnected.

'I must get back to the top table and put the smiles back on their faces,' Sarah said.

'Put the smile back on mine first, Sarah? Why? What's it all about?'

Sarah stood and smoothed down the dress. She raised her chin in an attitude that Alice could only think of as defiant. 'Because Tom has asked me to marry him and I said that I would.' She drew a thin ribbon from the neck of her dress. It was threaded through a ring bearing a single large diamond. 'He's going to announce it when he makes his speech.'

The first comment to spring to Alice's lips was hardly flattering. 'I don't believe it!' she said.

Sarah took the remark at face value. 'I still don't quite believe it myself,' she said. 'Don't look at me like that. I'm as surprised as you are. He was quite unnecessarily romantic about it. He took me out into the gardens to where we could see the south front framed in roses, and went down on one knee. I quite surprised myself by telling him that he didn't have to make the grand gesture and that I'd settle for going on as we are. But he doesn't want me as a mistress. It isn't because he's a sweet, old-fashioned thing, although he is, but he says that what he needs most in the world is a competent and businesslike partner who can also keep his remaining hormones in circulation and now that he's found her he wants some extra assurance that he can hang on to her.'

Alice jumped up, kissed Sarah and gave her a hug and then sat down again. 'But, Sarah—'

Sarah thought about sitting down beside her but changed her mind. Instead, she leaned back against the filing cabinet. 'I

282

know what you're going to say. Yes, I'll be a countess and I've made up my mind that I'll be a damned good one. I really do love that man. He's kind and he's cuddly and he's always polite and he never says an unkind word about anybody. That's the kind of man I could devote my life to.'

'But Sarah,' Alice said. She knew that she was repeating herself but repetition seemed to be inevitable. 'But Sarah, he must be – what? – thirty years older than you are at least.'

'He's twenty-two years older than I am. All right, so statistically in about another twenty-five years I could expect to become a dowager and stay that way for the next thirty, though nothing can lie like statistics. But I shan't forget my friends and I hope that they won't forget me.'

'But Sarah, what about ... I forget what I was going to say.'

'You were going to say, "What about when he gets past sex?" weren't you?' (Alice made a faintly negative sound but without real conviction. That had been exactly what she was going to say.) 'Well,' Sarah said, 'I dare say that I can live without it by that time of life. But if I'm as clever as I think I am, I shouldn't have to.'

Alice pulled her eyebrows down by muscular effort. 'I wish you every happiness in the world,' she said. 'And while you're remembering your humble friends, don't forget that one or two of us have been developing a certain knack for organizing weddings.' She looked at her new, jewel-encrusted watch. It was very difficult to read but she loved it all the same. 'Now we'd better move. I'm hungry and I want to hear the speeches.'

'No hurry,' Sarah said. 'With half the guests still scattered over the county and changing into dry clothes, this lunch is going to go on forever.'

'It's only costume jewellery,' Susan Evans said. She walked on towards the plane, almost dancing. Months of planning had gone into the coup, but when the time came it had proved almost too easy.

The official looked up from the X-ray machine. 'It looked more like telephone directories to me,' she said to the guard hovering beside the metal detector.